To: Nicki

Thank you for reading the book

Be Blessed
CJMCoop
12/15/2011

God Sent Us Angels In The Form of
GOOD WHITE FOLKS

God Sent Us Angels In The Form of
GOOD WHITE FOLKS

*Mama's Good
White Folks Angels*

CTM COOPER

WestBow
PRESS
A DIVISION OF THOMAS NELSON

Copyright © 2011 CTM Cooper

All rights reserved. No part of this book may be used or reproduced by any means, graphic, electronic, or mechanical, including photocopying, recording, taping or by any information storage retrieval system without the written permission of the publisher except in the case of brief quotations embodied in critical articles and reviews.

WestBow Press books may be ordered through booksellers or by contacting:

WestBow Press
A Division of Thomas Nelson
1663 Liberty Drive
Bloomington, IN 47403
www.westbowpress.com
1-(866) 928-1240

Because of the dynamic nature of the Internet, any web addresses or links contained in this book may have changed since publication and may no longer be valid. The views expressed in this work are solely those of the author and do not necessarily reflect the views of the publisher, and the publisher hereby disclaims any responsibility for them.

Certain stock imagery © Thinkstock.
Any people depicted in stock imagery provided by Thinkstock are models,
and such images are being used for illustrative purposes only.

ISBN: 978-1-4497-2145-9 (e)
ISBN: 978-1-4497-2144-2 (sc)
ISBN: 978-1-4497-2146-6 (hc)

Library of Congress Control Number: 2011911779

Printed in the United States of America

WestBow Press rev. date: 09/08/2011

Contents

Introduction	vii
A New Beginning	1
God Will Provide	9
Content Street	11
Homemade Toys	16
Witches Riding	18
Mama's First Friend in Jackson	20
The First Day of School	25
Blackballed	27
Mama Had to Go to Work	29
We Move to Carnation Street	32
Love Thy Neighbor	35
Baby Makes Nine	37
Heavenly Scent	40
Sister, Sister	42
Christmas 1959	44
The Maid's Grapevine	48
The Teen Years	54
Summer's End	56
Lanier Dear	59
The Movement	61
Good Men Dying	64
Like a Princess	68
Sissy's Return	71
The Metallic Bouffant Dress	73
Babies and More Babies	76
Life's Training Lessons	78
The Girdle Incident	80
Back to Leland	83

Chopping Cotton	87
Sweet Sixteen	91
Our Move to Newport Street	93
Brinkley Junior/Senior High	95
Mrs. Cole's Garden Party	97
The Nutmeg Incident	99
My Cup Was Full	101
Sudie Gray's	105
A Star is Born	107
Change in Mississippi	109
Daddy Found Jesus	113
Surprise….Surprise….Surprise	115
Jackson, Mississippi, 1967	118
I Saw Hate	121
My Return Home	125
Hard Times and Heartaches	148
If The Truth Be Told	153
"Man Of Honor	155
Giving Back	156
From Tot's and Mama's Cookbook	157
"A Tough Row To Hoe"	171
A Few Noted People from Mississippi According to Wikipedia	172

Introduction

When my mother and father's health began to fail, I took them both into my home to care for them. Mama still had her wits about her, but Daddy was having a rough time of it. He was diagnosed with Alzheimer's and could not accept the fact that he could no longer work. Many times I would have to stay up all night to make sure he would not leave the house.

After Daddy died in 2003, it was just me and my mother. Mama was sweet and funny. She would often reminisce about the white families she worked for and tell funny stories of different things that happened. One day she announced that she wanted to write a book about some of the people she really loved. In fact, she said, "Clem, I would like to write a book about Mrs. Cole, Mrs. Buford, Mr. Gene and Miss Tot." I told her that sounded like fun. Then she announced that she wanted to name it "God Sent Us Angels In The Form of Good White Folks". I told her that surely seemed like a mighty long title. But that is what she wanted and that's what I did. As she started to tell me some of the things that she and Mrs. Buford did together and some of the funny things that happened, I started to remember some of the things that I had experienced at her "Good White Folks Angels" homes. Some of my best memories were of Sissy and me dancing and all of the nice things the people my mother worked for had done for me. As Mama talked, more and more came to mind. It was as if a video camera were replaying all of those memories, as plain as day. It was like being in a divine dream state. As Mama talked and I wrote down the things she was saying, I pictured them in my mind. We would laugh and sometimes tears would come into her eyes and mine. It was the best of times and the worst of times sometimes for us, but God made it alright.

In Loving Memory Of The Author's Mother

Rosella Williams Thompson

Mrs. Rosella Williams Thompson, (Rosie) was born June 18, 1920, in the little Mississippi Delta town of Burdett, which you just can find on the map. She was the oldest daughter of Calvin Cannon and Erna Ida Williams Cannon. Raised by her grandmother, she carried the name of her grandparents. She married William Joseph Thompson in Greenville, Mississippi in 1937, with the permission of her grandmother. They moved to Hattiesburg, Mississippi where the first seven of their children were born. A cousin from Leland a small town in the Mississippi Delta came to visit them, bragging about how much money could be made sharecropping in the Delta. He had a large sum of money with him at the time.

Her husband decided to move their family to the Delta for a better life. After a bad sharecropping experience, they moved to Jackson in the winter of 1952, where God had prepared angels all around them to meet their needs and change their lives. I know, because I was there to see it all. Over the years of hardships and trials, she persevered to become a gifted cook, gardener, and collector of antique furniture and jewelry. She loved God with her whole heart. She was also a master of crewel embroidery and caring for her husband, children and, last not least, her "Good White Folks Angels", whom she loved.

My mother had a gift for storytelling, and she had a memory like an elephant. All of our family history came from the times we sat around daddy's and mama's feet listening, to different accounts of the life and lifestyles of our relatives of old. We had so many wonderful memories, some sad but also happy and extremely funny.

Author

Clementine Thompson Michael Cooper

(CTM) Cooper was born in a time, discrimination and segregation for blacks was widespread. Her family moved from the Mississippi Delta in 1952 to Jackson where she was educated. She is a mother, grandmother and former Associate Pastor of Living Waters Bible Fellowship Church.

This Book Is Dedicated To My Mother's Good White Folks Angels

In the early 1950's when we moved to Jackson, Mississippi, it was a large rural city with much larger buildings than we were accustomed to in Leland, the Mississippi Delta town from which we had moved. The art deco Standard Life Building and the fancy King Edwards Hotel were the tallest buildings downtown. At that time black people could not shop on Capitol Street, and all public buildings had signs on them to indicate where the "Colored" people could go to the bathroom or drink water. Separate but equal facilities were the words written in many local and state government documents. In the minds of many white officials, the Constitution was being followed to the letter. As one of our former Senators once said in the United States Senate, "the N's in Mississippi are as content as Carnation Cows".

Having said that, I want to tell you the story of my Mama and some of the white well-to-do families in Jackson, she called her "Good White Folks Angels", whose families adopted Miss Rosie as their very own. Much of what I have written in this book was dictated to me after my mother had grown old and was no longer able to work because of the onset of arthritis.

Mama said to me one day," Clem, I want you to write a book about Mrs. Buford, Mrs. Cole, Mr. Gene and Miss Tot." I said "That should be fun." She said "I want you to call it 'God Sent Us Angels

In The Form of Good White Folks.'" I laughed and said "That's a mighty long title." She said, "But that's just what they are to me – Good White Folks Angels."

While you are reading this book, keep in mind that mother was most honest in all her dealing with people. If she liked you, she liked you and if she loved you she went the last mile of the way with you.

The Good White Folks Angels

Mrs. Vera Buford

Mrs. Buford was a sophisticated, funny, well-groomed socialite with a heart of gold and a laugh that was full of joy. She had married well and had a career as a nurse. After she was widowed, she raised five daughters by herself. Her hobbies were playing bridge, traveling, cooking, and clothes – she was always dressed to the max and her hair done to perfection. She was a blessing to Mama, me, and our family as a whole.

Mrs. Jane Cole

Mrs. Cole was a devout Christian, full of life, small but mighty, with zeal, for all the beautiful things God had placed in her care on earth. She loved and cared for her husband, children, home, yard, and her Rosie Poise, as she called Mama. She truly had the compassion of Christ in her heart. She was active in the missions in her church and generous to those less fortunate. Giving to others seemed to give her great joy.

Mr. Eugene Yelverton, Jr.

Mr. Yelverton was Mama's movie star with a smile that would melt your heart. She told him one day while they were cooking in his kitchen that he was too pretty to be a man. She said he smiled and said "Aw Rosa, stop that" and they both laughed. Mr. Gene was soft spoken and always dapper, even in his sports clothes. God had put a very special spirit in him. He didn't say much, his actions spoke for him. He loved his wife, his children, his family and Mama. He enjoyed cooking, traveling, and caring for others. Mama loved him like one of her very own sons.

Mrs. Tot Bailey

Miss Tot had a soft spot in Mama's heart. She called her a Cinderella Doll. Mama said "She is like a little lamb. You know Miss Tot really knows God. When she hugs you, you just feel warm inside. God is always going to bless her." Miss Tot loved God, her husband, her children, her family and Mama. She asked Mama many years ago to partner with her in writing a cook book. They never got the opportunity. In memory of Mama's and Miss Tot's cook book, I added some of the recipes that they used to cook in this book.

(Sissy) Catherine Buford Fenoglio

Mama called Sissy her "Wild Child." Mama said Sissy just needed a lot of love, attention, and a good old fashioned spanking. Sissy was Scarlett O'Hara with an attitude, with a little Dennis the Menace on the side. She was a blond bombshell, pretty as a picture, with a smile wide as the Mississippi. She could have been the child spoken of in the song "summertime". She had nothing to cry about. Sissy lived the good life and enjoyed every day of it. She loved her family, dancing, traveling, decorating, dressing, and her Mama Rosie, and she is still one of my best friends.

Rose Budd Stevens

In the seventies and eighties mama had a pen pal she developed a special relationship with, although they never met in person. In honor of their faithful relationship as friends, I have added some of their communications such a letters, quilt patterns and recipes.

As Mama aged her arthritis became severe. She loved to read and sew. She found a column in our local newspaper, The Jackson Daily News called "Along the RFD" by Rose Budd Stevens. She drew much needed comfort and relaxation from it. My mother had many hobbies but I think that she loved reading most of all.

The articles and letters from Rose Budd gave Mama so much pleasure. In 1987 Mrs. Cole gave Mama an autographed copy of Rose Budd's book, "Along the RFD" which she treasured. Rose Budd's book was right up there by her stack of Bibles, books from Billy Graham, Oral Roberts and the Daily Devotional magazines that Mrs. Cole gave her every month.

Mama and Rose Budd communicated for years. What started out as a very casual correspondence turned out to be sharing family anecdotes about children, exchanging family accounts of personal experiences and just plain fun. Mama collected nearly every recipe that was published in Rose Budd's column.

The one thing all of Mama's "Good White Folks Angels" had in common was love - the God kind of love. That's what happens when God is present.

Special Acknowledgement

Suzanne Mathews

Special acknowledgment goes to one of my very own "Good White Folks Angels" God has always sent wonderful people into my life, such as my beloved friends Van and Penny Fergurson. We lost Van May 6, 2010 due to Lung Cancer. He was one of my very own Good White Folks Angels. Through them I met Penny's sister. A new caring faithful friend Suzanne Mathews who did the first edit of this book. She kept me grounded and encouraged me during the process. She has been added to my very own Good White Folks Angel list.

Suzanne would drive from Terry, Mississippi to pick up the manuscript to do correction and retype. She never asked for money or compensation of any kind. I asked her one day to let me at least give her gas money, which she refused. When God is in the plan, He will put people with the right kind of hearts in your path, to help carry out His Plan. I believe this book is ordained by God to show people of all walks of life, the true love and kindness that can happen between all races and all people when the God kind of love is present.

With much love and gratitude,
CTM Cooper

God Sent Us Angels In The Form Of Good White Folk

This first part of this book is dedicated to my wonderful grandchildren, who always let me know that they love me just because, and to my equally wonderful children Calvin, Joseph, Harrison, Heather, Rita, Tina and Zoe who love me just for me, and who gave me my beautiful grandchildren. This story is for family history and documentation of your roots. Many times we as parents in this modern society forget to tell the stories of ancestors of old. We forget the family traditions, the life changing experiences and the impact of knowing historical facts of your heritage that could very well change the destiny of many of our children lives.

There is a spiritual song that states *"We ought to all go back to the old time way."* The way we use to serve and depend on God tells the stories that help us remember how we got over all of the hurt, pain, oppression and injustice blacks suffered from the time we were brought to the new world. Doing those times we leaned and depended on the Lord God All Mighty to see us through. I believe what the composer was trying to convey in this song is that sometimes we need to look back at our past and just do the things that we know are the right things to do, according to God's Word. Many times as I looked back, I'm grateful for the many opportunities that I had. The life lessons that I learned through hardships, heartbreaks, failures and successes. The lessons that I learned were from the loving kindness that was shown to me by the most unlikely people that I would've thought had my best interest and concern in mind. The Bible tells us to entertain strangers. In doing so we may have entertained angels. Never forget where you came from because if you forget where you came from, surely you won't know where you're going. We must build our life on things eternal. This simply means never forget that it is God who has kept and girded us up in every situation of our lives. We need to remember the Golden Rule, "Do unto others as you would have them do unto you." As my mother's "Good White Folks Angels" did.

A Word of Thanks

I am thankful to my granddaughters who helped type and edit and my darling prayer partners who are also my dear friends, who lifted me up in prayer daily as I wrote the book. Without them I may have just stop writing. I inherited mother's Osteoarthritis and sometimes my fingers just would not bend to let me type. But by the Grace of God and the kind act of my son Joseph, who bought me a "speak and type" program for my computer and the prayers of my pastor and friends, I pressed on. I would also like to thank Pastor Calvin J. Michael II, Ms. Ruby F. Hendricks, Mrs. Christine McCurtis, Evangelist Carolyn Spann, Enrique and Lizzie Diaz and Mrs. Pamela Tillman- Brown. May God continue to bless you all.

To my sisters: Rosa, Willie Ruth, Dorothy, Cecilia, and Donna thank you for your support and love.

Be Blessed.

A New Beginning

I was born in July 1948, the fifth of nine children, born to William Joseph and Rosella Thompson. That was the year the Jews went home, television came on the scene, bread was fourteen cents for a 1-pound loaf and minimum wage was 40 cents an hour. President Harry S. Truman asked congress to outlaw lynching, and to establish a Civil Rights Commission. Black people were "colored". Some of the facts in this paragraph were taken from a birthday card, given to me by my baby sister.

Daddy and Mama were married five years before they had children. Mama often spoke of how Daddy prayed everyday that God would give them children, but what Daddy didn't know was when God started giving him children, He almost didn't know when to stop.

The first seven of their nine children were born in Hattiesburg, Mississippi. I don't remember much about Hattiesburg and I don't remember leaving there. But as I listened to Daddy and Mama talk about where we had lived and the experiences they had, certain things came to mind. I remember when I got my ears pierced at age four and that I was so scared. I could see the lady heating a sewing needle with a match until the sharp end was fire red. Then she dipped the burned point of the needle in alcohol. The eye of the needle was threaded with white thread. She got a cork and some alcohol with which she rubbed my ear lobe, and pushed the needle in at the front, until the thread came out the back and made a loop in the thread and tied it. That's how we got our ears pierced. I remember a little about going to church in Hattiesburg, because Daddy always took us to church no matter where we were.

Daddy and Mama were good people but poor. There is nothing to explain about poor, but on the other hand maybe there is, because there are degrees of poor. Some people are working class poor, some are dirt poor, some are poorer than dirt poor, and that poor is sleeping-in-a-cardboard-box-poor, God forbid. We were in that working poor classification.

Our poor was somewhere between living in one room of a rooming house, with the toilet in the hall, or a house with the toilet enclosed in a closet-sized room on the back porch. When you went in to use the bathroom, you had to sit sideways so your knees would not touch the wall in front of you. There were three to four children to a bed, and yes, we had that wonderful government cheese, powdered eggs, powdered milk, and don't let me forget the peanut butter and canned meat known as commodities, that kept most black folks alive. We were on the Adkins Diet and did not even know it.

Rosa, my oldest sister, Daddy and Mama's first born, said we moved from Hattiesburg in 1951. Daddy had a 1942 black Ford car that he packed us all in, two deep. Cars back then were not roomy like automobiles are today, so some of the smaller children had to sit on the older children's laps all the way to Grand mama's house. Two adults and seven children – we were moving to Leland Mississippi, up in the Mississippi Delta. That's where my mother's people lived including Mama's mother, Mama Erna, great grandmother Eveline Williams, my Aunt Luella, and her husband Uncle Horse Davis, and my great aunt Elnora Green, Mama Erna's older sister. We were around my mother's family more than Daddy's because most of Daddy's people migrated north, except the few in Hattiesburg and New Orleans but most of Mama's lived in Mississippi. All of Mama's family seemed to love Daddy. He was "The Man" of both families. I think that's why Daddy thought he might do well at farming cotton in the Delta.

I remember more about the Delta than Hattiesburg, because I was a little older when we got to Leland. It was early spring and the weather was very pleasant.

We stayed with Mama Erna and Great grandma Eveline Williams on Main Street. The house was right on the main highway. It was as if Highway 61 turned into Main Street. As we drove up the big white house jumped out at you. Boy what a sight. There was a long front porch that had a swing on it hanging from the ceiling on big chains. The right front window was round like an old English cottage with tall windows. It was kind of spooky, in a horror movie sort of way.

We were here, and all the kinfolk seemed happy to see us, but to my surprise there were no children to be found. None of Mama's close relatives had children, not a one. My Aunt Luella was married but she and Uncle Horse Davis had no children. We were only there for a short time and they let us know that they didn't like children messing up. That is probably why God didn't give them any children. We had to sit outside most of the day. After breakfast or lunchtime we were outside until time to go to bed.

But I must say that all of Mama's female family members sure could cook. We had wonderful food, and fun outside eating it. On Fridays and Saturdays we sat on the porch and waited for the Hot Tamale Man to come by. He rolled his cart down the sidewalk and yelled "Hot Tamales, Hot Tamales" as loud as he could and one of the adults sitting on the porch, went out to the sidewalk and bought some for us. That was such fun. Those hot tamales sure were good. We had so many wonderful things close around us.

Mr. Arthur Forbes store was about two doors down from my grandmother's house. We walked to the store in the evenings, where we bought Dixie Cup ice cream and whatever ten cents would buy, which at that time, was a lot. For a penny you could get two big Jack's Moon Cookies, as we called them because they were as large as pancakes and Stage Planks that tasted like gingerbread. We could

3

buy a nickel's worth of Red Rind cheese, to go with our cookies and we could eat all day. Most all individual candy and bubble gum were two for a penny so a dime went a long way.

After dusk when the sun was down, one of the elders would make a smoke, that warded off the mosquitoes and other bugs. They put some old rags in a pan and set them on fire. After the rags started to burn the elder put the flame out, and the rags began to smoke up the area where we were sitting. Then all the ladies fixed their dip of Garrett Snuff in the corner of their lips, at the bottom and the story telling of Ancestors of Old began. While we were listening to the stories we heard the sounds of the bullfrogs in Deer Creek, and the background chorus of crickets and locusts in the trees. That was the only time the children could sit among the grown folk. Jim Henson, the creator of the Muppets, said in an interview once that he got his character, Kermit the Frog from the bullfrogs he played with on the banks of Deer Creek in Leland, which was his home.

My personal favorite story of all was about the 1927 flood when the levee broke at Greenville. That story would make the hair stand up on your arms and the back of your neck. My mother was seven years old when the storms and steady rains came through the Mississippi Delta. Mama said, "The winds mounted up like tornadoes and people, houses and cattle were swept away for miles by the flood waters." I began to understand why Mama was so afraid of storms, as she spoke of the odors and the sight of dead bodies, human and animal, floating in the high waters. She said the smell was horrible, enough to make you sick. Mama and her grandmother, who had raised her from a small child, had already been taken to higher ground before the water got too high. Mama heard some time later that they were on top of some Indian mounds.

Mama Erna was working on a river boat as a cook during that time, and she would bring food to them when she came home in the evening. After they ate Great Grandma Eveline Williams, a devout Church of God Saint, lit the coal oil lamp and searched in her Bible to make sure, God was not destroying the evil people on earth again by water, as he had done in the time of Noah. Great Grandma was sure sin had something to do with what was happening there with such destruction taking place. She thought surely a curse was on the Mississippi Delta, and the sins of the fathers were being visited on their sons for their wickedness and they all were being punished. No matter how many times I heard the account of the Great Flood of 1927, I always learned something new, and Mama kept telling the story for many years.

A short time after we had gotten to the Delta, Daddy found a sharecropping farm a few miles outside of Leland. The farm was south of Leland going back down 61 Highway. I don't know how many acres it was, but you could see cotton for what seemed like miles, row after row as far as the eye could see. It was late spring and it was time to chop the grass and vines from around the cotton. The older children whose ages ranged from 8 to 10 and Daddy and Mama worked in the field.

Late Friday evening we went to my grandmother's house in town. We would visit our aunts and uncles. Sometimes we all went downtown. You could hear the music coming from the cafes. Fish and chicken were frying and people were laughing and dancing and having big fun.

We stayed at my grandmother's house until Sunday evening and then headed back to the sharecropping farm. By the time we got to the farm it was time for us to go to bed. The next morning Daddy would get up before everybody and light a fire in the wood-burning stove, to warm the house up. At the crack of dawn, Mama and the four older children would get up, and get ready to go to the cotton field. Mama or Willie Ruth made biscuits for breakfast and Daddy would get the can of Brer Rabbit molasses and sit it on the table. While the biscuits were cooking, fat meat or bacon was frying, and the smell was wonderful. The younger children were still under the heavy quilts to keep warm from the chill of the morning.

Willie Ruth, my next to the oldest sister, stayed home with the younger children while Daddy, Mama, Rosa and the older boys went to the cotton field. At straight up 12:00 o'clock noon everybody came home for lunch. Willie Ruth had lunch ready. I remember this really good tomato gravy with rice and biscuits she made. The tomatoes grew wild beside the house. We called them bird tomatoes, because they were so small and sweet. That was a good hot lunch. After lunch sometimes Daddy let me help him pump the water, from the pump on the side of the house. Daddy showed me how to prime the pump, to make the water start to run out of the pump spout, to fill the water bucket so they would have water to carry back to the field.

When it was time to go back to the field when it was cotton picking time Daddy often told how, I was riding on his cotton sack until it got too heavy, while he was picking cotton. Daddy could pick two hundred pounds of cotton a day. He worked so hard. He would be so tired when he got home sometimes he was too tired to eat. As I think back, he might have been waiting to let the children and Mama eat first.

Daddy tried his best at sharecropping, but it just didn't work out. Daddy, Mama and my older brothers and sisters had worked in the fields chopping weeds all spring and picking cotton all summer. For all his months of toil and labor Daddy did not make one dime. All that work was for nothing! The owner of the sharecropping farm where we lived in the shanty shack, with all that cotton around it, said daddy owed most of the money to his store, for food and supplies and for the time we had lived in the shack. I guess, you know, Daddy was pretty mad as well as disappointed. And that's how Daddy decided to move us to Jackson, the capital city. Daddy had good jobs in Hattiesburg, which was considered a big city. He must have thought a bigger city would be even better to find a good job.

When we moved to Jackson, it must have been December 1952 because it wasn't very long until it was Christmas. Daddy had moved us into a rooming house on the corner of Mill and Cohea Streets in one room, with a wood-burning stove. You had to go in the hall to go to the bathroom. I think it was colder in the hall than it was outside. To this very day I have a special love for beautiful inside bathrooms.

That's right – one room with nine people living in it, seven children and two parents. It was the dead of winter and there was no heat. As a matter of fact we had no utilities and no food. Mama, who I admired for her survival skills, made hoecakes in a big black skillet that was sitting on some coals in the stove in the corner of the big room. For those of you who are not familiar with hoecakes they are like pancakes made with corn meal instead of flour. We lived off of hoecakes all the time we were at the rooming house. We did all right; mama kept us alive. Daddy had not found work, but I don't remember any one complaining about what we were going through.

Late at night when mama thought we were all asleep, I would see her over by the stove reading her grandmother's bible. Some time I could see tears streaming down her face. Mama was having a hard time seeing her children suffer; she would bow her head and pray. She had to be praying to God, that daddy would soon find work, so we could move out of that one room. I was just thankful that the toilet was indoors because on that cotton farm the toilet was outside, in what mama and daddy called an outhouse. My older sisters would take us to the outhouse, I was always afraid that I was going to fall in. Thank God I never did, I liked the chamber pot better, but you could only use it at night in the house.

So all in all we still had something to be happy about. We had a roof over our heads and at least we had something to eat. I think the way we lived back then made us appreciate everything that God provided for us the more. When we lived in Leland at my grandmother's, the outhouse was at the very back of the back yard pass the henhouse. My grandmother had this rooster in the backyard that I declare was possessed. It didn't matter what reason you were in the backyard, the plumage on the back of his neck would rise, and he would start to run after you. I absolutely hated him, because I loved getting the eggs out of the henhouse, and many times when I had to go to the outhouse (bathroom) I would just hold it. He indeed, made my life a bit more difficult to say the least. So in fact, I could thank God that we just had to go in the hall to the bathroom, and I didn't have to deal with a rooster.

When you are a little child you don't have to think about a lot, and you can adapt to most any situation. One thing is all so apparent, you can feel when things are going right or wrong with your parents. You can see happiness and joy or you could see sadness and despair in their eyes. I looked in my parent's eyes and I saw sadness and despair every day.

The Shanty Shack On
The Sharecropping Farm Outside of Leland, Mississippi

God Will Provide

We had not been living in Jackson long as I recall when Daddy got up one morning and went walking. A short time later he came back. He "told us to get up and get dressed." Mama and the older girls got us dressed and Daddy took us to a church around the corner, where Morning Star Baptist Church was at that time. After singing some Christmas carols and a short program, a group of people asked all of the children to stand and walk around a long table. They gave us all a brown paper bag, with a red or green bow wrapped around the top of it. When I opened my bag, there was a big red apple, a navel orange, nuts, and peppermint candy canes in it. What a blessing! I was so happy, all I can say is something is better than nothing. That was all we had for Christmas that year. "Thank you Lord."

I don't remember how long we stayed on Cohea Street. However I do remember Mama saying during family reminiscing that while we lived there, Daddy went out every day looking for work. He came home one day and said he needed a reference for a company that he had applied for work. Mama wrote a letter to the company in Hattiesburg, where Daddy had worked for many years. They gave daddy a very good reference to the company where he had applied. Daddy got the job and started working for McCarty/Holman's Wholesale Grocery Company. They owned the Jitney Grocery Stores in Mississippi and some surrounding southern states.

God has always sent us Guardian Angels, in the form of "Good White Folks" who were filled with an abundance of compassion. One thing about God, He always overpowers evil with good. Mama taught me that all people are not alike and there is some good and some evil people in all cultures and races, which is why to this very day, I treat everyone the way I would like to be treated, white, black, or other.

Old Morning Star MB Church
From first Christmas in Jackson

Content Street

After Daddy got the job at McCarty Holman's, we moved to Content Street by the Jackson Ready-Mix Cement Company. We moved into a beautiful duplex apartment, what some people might call a shotgun apartment because all the rooms were in a straight line and you could stand in the front door and shoot a shotgun right out the back door. We had inside plumbing and all the utilities were on, lights, gas and water. What a blessing!

On Content we started our move up. We had food from the grocery store, and treats that they gave Daddy at work that he brought home to us. This was the good life, compared to our Cohea Street experience. We even got our first television set. Our family was the only family in the neighborhood to have one. That was something. After Daddy and Mama finished watching the evening news my older brother William Alfred and I watched the Grand Ole Opry on Friday nights and went in the front yard to square dance. I could certainly doe-si-doe. I guess that's how my love of dancing started. We also watched "Amos and Andy" and late Saturday night we watched "The Squeaking Door." Staring Boris Karioff

Sometimes we watched the Friday Night Fights with Daddy. He sure did enjoy the fights. Daddy taught me how to appreciate sports, and that's good for a girl. We all sat on the floor around Daddy's feet watching TV. Mama was in bed watching television with us. I loved those times; I even loved watching the wonderful commercials back then. The Speedy Alka-Seltzer boy was my favorite.

On Saturday mornings I watched the cartoons, and the cowboy and cowgirl shows that came on. There was Wild Bill Hickcok and Annie Oakley, Roy Rogers and Dale Evans with the Sons of the Pioneers, and The Lone Ranger and his Indian sidekick Tonto. I loved all of them but Dale Evans was my favorite. I got a cowgirl hat and a stick horse for Christmas one year, along with a cap pistol with paper caps and a holster. The only thing missing was a real horse.

I also liked the Howdy Doody Show with Buffalo Bob. They were having a contest to win a Shetland pony. All you had to do was send in a postcard, with your name and address on it, and it went into a drawing. Mama sent my postcard in for me. I waited and waited for the drawing. That Saturday morning finally came and as they rolled the big drum with all the cards in it, my heart almost stopped. After turning the drum round and round, Buffalo Bob got a child from the audience to put his hand in the drum opening. He pulled out a card and read the name. It wasn't mine. I was so hurt I said to myself, "One day I will buy my own pony." I still watched the show but I never did enter another contest.

I liked living in our apartment. It seemed to give us a closeness that made me feel secure. Our living room was what you might call, a living room/bedroom combination, because our family was large and daddy could not afford better housing for us at the time. Most duplex apartments had only one bedroom, Mama made ours the "mother-in-law" plan, – children in the back and grownups in the front. When we had company, our room became the guestroom, and the children slept on the floor. Mama piled lots of quilts on the floor and made an instant king-sized bed. I didn't mind because the covers were always so very clean. They had the fresh clean smell of outdoors.

Our neighborhood was a small area between the Jackson Ready-Mix Concrete Company and Pleasant Avenue. Content Street was paved around 2007 but it is still a narrow street with duplex shotgun apartments and ours is still there.

As time passed we started to attend Bertha Chapel Baptist Church not far from our house. We could walk to church on Sundays. I was only six years old but there were certain things I remember. I went to church mostly with my older sisters. I was fascinated with the piano player (back then we didn't call them musicians). I don't remember her name but, sometimes she let me sit on the piano stool beside her while she was getting her songs ready for Sunday service. When the service started she played "Do Lord, Do Lord Do Remember Me" I felt all warm inside, especially when she got to the part that said "I got a home in Glory Land that outshines the sun." The singing and music were the best parts of the service to me.

Mama and Daddy must have been happy during that time because Mama had – you guessed it – another baby. It was April 1954 that's when my knee baby brother, Anthony was born. Let me explain what the knee baby of the family is. The knee baby is the baby born before the last child is born. This is a fact according to my mother, who was always right.

Anyway, the day my mother was coming home from the hospital, my older sisters Rosa and Willie Ruth were cleaning all morning. There was such a business in the house. They cleaned for what seemed like hours and then Daddy said "I am going to get your Mama." All I know is that house was so clean that it seemed as if a chill was in there. Mama's bed was as white as the driven snow, just the way she liked it. She had a thing about her bed; no one, and I mean no one, could ever sit on Mama's bed.

Willie Ruth and Rosa had even bathed the younger children. We were shining, Vaseline from head to toe. I still did not realize what the fuss was all about, but around noon a big black hearse pulled up to the front door. Man, was I scared! I had never seen anything like that. Of course, I didn't know that the vehicle was a hearse until later after hearing Mama and Daddy talking. Two men got out and went to the back of the vehicle and opened the door and pulled out what looked like a bed on wheels, and Mama was on it. Seeing Mama on that narrow bed made things a little better, but she had what looked like a basket with a bundle in it. The men brought Mama in the house and she got in her bed with the bundle. At first I thought it was a doll, but it was moving so I figured that it was not a doll. After it started moving and crying, Mama asked one of my older sisters to warm the baby's bottle, after that I knew for sure it was a baby. That is how I found out that babies are brought home in big long black cars. Later I learned that Daddy didn't have a car, so he got his good friend Mr. Walter Steward at People's Funeral Home on Farish Street to bring Mama home for him. My sisters put an oval bassinet in the living room by Mama's bed. Our living room was the master bedroom and living room combination, and that's where Mama and the baby were, but that was still better than living in one room as we had on Cohea Street.

Daddy always worked hard but somehow, he always came up short. He just couldn't make it with what he earned, having a wife and eight children to take care of, no matter what job he had. He may not have had lots of money, but he had lots of love for his wife and children. We were blessed because we had a father and a mother and a real sense of family. Black men have in many cases gotten a bad rap for not providing for their families, but the truth of the matter is most black men in my father's day were closed out of good paying jobs. However most of them stayed and did the best they could with what they had to provide for their families.

I know it had to be painful to go day after day, knowing that your family was in need of the very basic life-sustaining needs knowing that you're the head of the house -hold. A man willing to work and not being able to find work that would pay you enough to take care of your family, that had to be heartbreaking and stressful.

Cohea Street Rooming House

Homemade Toys

Most of the time, we just socialized with each other. Mama always said there were just enough of us to entertain each other. We didn't play with the neighborhood children, mainly because Mama wouldn't let us. She considered most children heathens and she didn't want us to act like them. We had neighborhood children next door to us, but Poochy and Sugar Baby were off limits. We only had sibling interaction mostly all through our early childhood. Only if cousins came to visit did we get a break from each other. It seemed to me that the sisters and brothers were paired off. I had two sisters and two brothers older than me and two sisters and two brothers younger than me. That put me smack dab in the middle, and much of the time I was alone but not lonely.

You see I had a wonderful imagination. I loved to play paper dolls or house in the back yard. I made mud cakes, cooked grass greens, and played with straw headed coca cola bottle dolls. We made those dolls from clear 8 ounce light green glass coke bottles. We took some straw yarn, stuck it in the top of the bottle, and put a cork or whatever would hold the straw in tight so that you could unbraid the straw, because then you had hair. Most colored children had to do that because our parents weren't able to replace the dolls we had gotten for Christmas if they melted or broke. So we made our own dolls and toys and repaired them. I don't know what our dolls back then were made of, but they would melt. Of course I didn't know that until I tried to give a doll I got for Christmas a bath. She was sitting there looking at me with one side of her face melted. She was such a fright she looked like Chuckie, the evil doll. I didn't want her looking at me so I put her in the bottom of the garbage can and away she went. If you were fortunate enough to get a pair roller skates for Christmas, and they wore out doing the year you would simply take the rollers, off of the skate and make you a scooter. You needed two long flat wood board's one for the foot board one for handle and a short T board. God gave us talent, creativity and patients, and we counted it all joy.

Witches Riding

If you had bad dreams, the elders called the experience "Witches Riding You". I don't know if witches were riding me or not but when I was a little girl about 6 to 8 years old, I dreamed a lot. One of my dreams was that I could shrink down to a size small enough to fit in a die cast matchbox car. I always had beautiful cars. Another recurring dream I had was a big black cat, something like a leopard, was after me, but just before he leaped to get me. I was able to spring up very high out of his reach. Sensing that he couldn't reach me, he would retreat. You better believe I was thrilled the dream turned out that way. Sometimes if I was in a deep sleep, it seemed as if a weight would start at my feet and slowly creep up my body. The heaviness would come up to my chest. In a flash I would wake up and could not get back to sleep. Sometimes I would go and get in bed with mama and daddy because I was so afraid. The best part about that is they would let me.

As I aged the recurring dreams became less frequent and finally stop altogether. Instead of witching riding I prefer to believe what daddy told me about the meaning of the dream. He said that God was showing me that I could rise above any bad thing that could happen to me in life. That concept remains with me to this very day.

Daddy seemed to always know how to put everything in proper perspective. There was a certain time of day that you could tell a person about a dream that you had. When I told daddy about my dream, so he could interpret it for me and he told me that my dream meant that no matter how hard a situation would be in my life, that God will always make me a way out for my good success. I took daddy at his word and so for, life has proven to be just as he said. Thanks be to God.

Mama's First Friend in Jackson

Things were going well and Mama seemed happy. She didn't have any friends that I can remember except, this one lady next door to us. Her name was Miss Lizzie. She was a dark-skinned lady with a very nice smile. Miss Lizzie and Mama sat and talked and had good visits. They talked about sewing and growing flowers while they drank coffee. I know because most of the time I was at home pretending to be sick so I didn't have to go to school

Mama was kind of anti-social and very scornful. You could almost say she had excessive-compulsive behavior, when it came to cleanliness. But for some reason she liked Miss Lizzie. Maybe it was because Miss Lizzie was clean too. They became friends planting flowers in the front yard. That's a fact according to my sister Rosa. That's what they did in the mornings – plant flowers and drink coffee. They had the prettiest flowers in that front yard.

When Miss Lizzie left our house to go home, Mama always sterilized the sofa or chair where she sat. Daddy had to buy a sofa and chair every other year or so because Mama faded all the cushions with Clorox cleaning up behind visitors.

Miss Lizzie and her husband didn't have children. I think that's why she liked us so much. I remember whenever it stormed, if Daddy wasn't home, Mama took us next door to Miss Lizzie's, because she was so afraid of bad weather.

During that period Daddy was sometimes given to strong drink. Or in other words he was sometimes a weekend drunk. If he came home in his habit, as mama called it, to Miss Lizzie's house we went until Daddy slept his habit off. Mama didn't like storms and she didn't like drunken people either.

Most of the time when we got home, Daddy was alright, everything would be back to normal. I always hoped that the night Daddy chose to get in his habit would be Saturday, because if he drank that day, he would not drink on Sunday because he wanted to be in good shape for work on Monday. Daddy tried to make up for his bad behavior by doing something sweet for Mama. He made Sunday dinner with all the fixings. He could cut up a whole chicken into sixteen pieces before you could say "Jack Sprat". He made the best creamed potatoes, rolls and string beans in the world, and for desert homemade banana pudding. I can almost taste it now. Everything was so good. Mama didn't say much, but I could sense she was still not pleased with Daddy, but after a while she would get all right. I know it was hard on Mama; many women today would have just left. I am glad God gave her the strength to stay.

While we were on Content Street, I started school and that's when my life changed. I had always been home with Mama. I had a very sheltered life. I hated the very idea of having to leave home. I had only been around my sisters and brothers. Every time I heard Mama and Daddy talking about school I felt sick. The only thing I got excited about was getting new clothes and shoes. Mama had this big Sears and Roebuck Catalog that she let us look through and pick out a few things to wear. Those were our school clothes for the year. The girls could get two pairs of shoes and three dresses. The boys could get 2 pairs of jeans, 3 shirts and one pair of shoes. Daddy and Mama had five school age children. We couldn't get much because there were so many of us to buy for.

Mama made some of our clothes by hand, a few things to go along with the clothes she ordered. Blacks couldn't shop at stores in downtown Jackson on Capital Street. For that reason mama ordered out of the Sears and Roebuck Catalog. There were some black owned businesses on Farish Street where we could shop, but we didn't have transportation. Mama always wanted us to look nice and clean. She said "You can be anything but nasty", which meant you must always keep your body and clothes clean as well your home.

Finally the day came and Mama sent the Sears order off. We were so excited! This was the first time we had gotten new clothes in a long while. And I know we had not gotten clothes since we had moved to Jackson.

In late August, the mailman delivered a very large cardboard box to our house. We were certainly happy as Mama opened the box. We all sat lined up on the sofa just smiling. Mama was smiling too. She was so proud to have clothes for her children. As she opens the box, she began to pull our different items out of the box, to match the items to each child. She had to order list in her hand, then she placed each pile in a line to match each child. Mama turned as she called each child by name, we would come and get our clothes and shoes, and try the on. Mama made sure she got the clothes a size or two too large so they would last all the school year.

We didn't have a lot of clothes. The ones we had all hung in the same small area in the back bed room behind the door. When daddy came home we were so excited. Mama took him to the back room, to show him our clothes. Daddy smiled and said to mama "you did good." But that wasn't all; mama had ordered daddy two shirts and two pairs of pants. He told her she shouldn't have done that. Mama wanted daddy to know that he was appreciated. All the time daddy had been working he had not gotten anything for himself, he was just like that. He always wanted to make sure mama and the children had what they needed. Sometimes I wonder if some of daddy's behavior, the drinking and short temper was attributed to some of the strains and stresses that he went through, not being able to provide better for his family the way he wanted to . He never complained, he just accepted the fact that he had to provide

God Sent Us Angels In The Form of Good White Folks

the best that he knew how, by whatever means necessary barring breaking the law.

Well we all were happy, my older brothers and sisters were very excited about school starting. I however was just excited about getting new clothes, just the word school made me feel uneasy. To think that I had to leave home, my safe haven to be around all those people just made me want to go and hide.

I think my oldest brother could sense that something was wrong with me. Mama had asked him to go to the store for her. He looked at me and asked me if I wanted to walk with him to the store. I said okay. He got the note and money from mama and we headed out the door. He looked at me as we were walking and asked me what was wrong. I told him that I didn't think I was going to like going to school. He smiled and said "school is fun. You get to meet friends, go outside to play, and you get to learn to read." I told him I can go outside to play at home with mama, she could teach me to read, and I don't like other children, I just like my sisters and brothers. He told me that most children feel like that when they first start school. He said he felt the same way, but as time passed and he got older, he begins to like school. I told him I would give it a try.

By the time we got through talking about school, we had made it to the store. Mama had sent at some Purex bleach. During that time Purex bleach came in dark brown glass bottles. Mama let me wear my new brown penny loafers to the store. Daddy would always put me two shinny new pennies in the slats on top of my loafers. I was holding the Purex bleach and didn't know that the cap was not tightly closed and some of the bleach got on my new loafers. I was sick. There on the top of my loafers were two light spots. I was so afraid that I was in trouble; I actually had a knot in my stomach. When we got home, I had tears in my eyes. Daddy was sitting on the porch. He looked at me and asked me what was wrong. I told him about the bleach spilling on my shoes. He said, "Those little spots, I'll just put some liquid shoe polish on those." That should fix them right up. I sure was glad daddy knew how to fix most anything. Well my brother had talked me into trying school. As if I had a choice, I knew that mama and daddy were going to make go whither I wanted to or not. Sometimes when daddy was reading the Bible to us he would make sure he read the passage from Proverbs 4:7 "Wisdom is the principal thing: Therefore get wisdom. *And in all your getting get understanding."* (Holy Bible -King James Version Red-Letter Edition) My parents knew that if I didn't get wisdom, knowledge would not come. I knew deep down I needed to go to school and as my brother said it would be alright.

The First Day of School

In the fifties and sixties, school started in September after Labor Day. I was in the first grade and I can tell you right now, I did not like it at all. The elementary school I attended was Mary C. Jones on Whitfield Mill Road, which is now Martin Luther King Drive. The first morning the teacher assigned everyone a cubbyhole to keep our books and supplies in, and then she assigned us desks according to the first initial of our last names.

We all got seated, and that's when it happened. The teacher stood at her desk, picked up her roll book and announced, "As I call your name, please stand and tell us a little about yourself". My stomach felt as though a ten-ton weight had been placed on it. When she called my name, I stood and said "My name is Clementine Thompson. I am six years old," and that was it.

I had never spoken in public before, and I was praying to God that I would never have to again. I hated school!! It made me uncomfortable from the first to the sixth grade. Many days I pretended to be ill, so I would not have to go to school. I was left back in the first grade because I didn't attend school enough days to pass, and that was alright with me. (Good ole mom)

You see, the schools I attended seemed to breed these teachers for the bottomless pit, yes **(H---)**. I remember every Friday we had to spell the words from our spelling book. We had to stand and recite the words from memory. One bad experience I remember was in fourth grade. I miss spelled Mediterranean Sea and a few other words. That teacher came over to me, and she bent the palm of my little hand back, and hit me as hard as she could with a paddle. The tears just streamed down my face. I not only suffered physical pain, but the shame was just as painful. After that experience I really didn't want to go back to school that made me hate school all the more. Somehow I did just enough to get promoted each year. I was promoted on to the fifth grade still not reading or spelling well, and I know it was God who got me through math.

As you can see school was not my best suit, but there were some good memories. Many times when walking from school in late spring, daylilies grew in a field on the path walking home. I would stop and pick my mother a bouquet of flowers. It made me feel good to be able to bring her something nice home. She would smile and say thank you, which made me feel so good.

We must have stayed on Content Street six years. We really enjoyed our stay there. It was nice with Daddy having steady work. Mama stayed home and cared for the children, just as Daddy liked it. We did not have a lot of frills and luxuries, just the basic necessity, and sometimes those were slim. But we were all happy with what was provided for us.

One day my sister Rosa, and I were reflecting on the past and she stated that, to her it didn't seem as if we were poor during that time, because most of the black families we lived around, during that time were living at or about, the same economic level as we were. The people on our street that lived better than us had study work and the husbands and wives both worked. Mama didn't work because she was home with her children, of course that made it harder on daddy he had to carry the burden of providing for the family himself. One thing I am sure of is I never heard any complaint.

Blackballed

Late one afternoon two men came to our house to talk with Daddy. When they left, Mama asked Daddy what they wanted. Daddy said they were trying to get a union for them at work. He told her that might get the workers more money and some benefits. I didn't know what a union was, but if Daddy was working to get one for the company, I was all for it. Little did I know this would bring another change for our family.

I didn't know that people at Daddy's company wouldn't like what Daddy and the other men were doing, getting a union. But shortly after all that union talk Daddy came home looking really down. He said he had been laid off from work. Daddy always had a progressive mind but this time his good deed had gotten him in trouble. He tried to keep in good spirits but it was hard. Daddy always had high hopes. He would say "I'll find another job soon." He went looking for work day after day, but he found nothing.

One day one of the men who were working with Daddy came by our house. I was sure that Daddy thought he was coming to tell him that he was getting his job back. When he left, Daddy came in and told Mama that the man said that Daddy had been **blackballed**. I didn't know what that meant but it didn't sound like it was good. When I got older I found out that blackball meant when you went to apply for a job with employers, if the former employer would not give you a good recommendation. And that would block you from getting hired with any other companies. Daddy had a strange distant look on his face, he was devastated. He went back outside and sit down and just stared out in space, I guess he was trying to figure out what was he going to do. He was disheartened but he knew he had to carry on. Later on daddy came in the house and announced to mama, well the same God that gave that job will give me another one.

Mama Had to Go to Work

Shortly after that Mama went out looking for work. She was unskilled but, for her time, she had good basic knowledge. She had an eighth grade education, and a whole lot of common sense, which was the standard for her era. She could read, write, spell, and count. Some children with a twelfth grade education nowadays can't do as well.

She started to do domestic private home work. When she would go to work, my older sisters would care for us. Her first job was working for Mrs. O'Quinn, a white lady who lived off Bailey Avenue. Many whites lived in that area back then.

That seemed to work out well for Mama because she had to walk to work. It was good that she found something close to home. She worked a few days a week for Mrs. O'Quinn, which helped with the rent and food, but with Daddy not working it was hard. Sometimes if the utilities were due, she had to cut back on food. Sometimes a utility would get cut off. One time our gas was cut off. It was very cold and Mama put some coals in a pan to burn to make heat. The coals started to smoke up the house. We were all asleep. By the time Daddy got home we had gotten carbon monoxide sick. If he had not gotten home in time, we would all have died. Daddy felt so bad he knew he had to do something. He tried harder to find work. He finally decided to work for himself.

Daddy started his own business doing lawn service. He got a contract to clean the yards and houses once people moved out of them. We were happy because Daddy was back working. He took all of us to work with him. The girls helped clean the inside of the houses, and the boys did the mowing and cleaned the yards.

Daddy's vehicles seemed to be from the Flintstone era because they ran by foot. We had to push them to get them started. If you can imagine five or six children behind a car or truck pushing it, that was us. Rain, shine, sleet, or snow, if Daddy had to go to work and that vehicle wouldn't start, we had to push it. To help get it started, I hated that. I would always say to myself, "When I grow up and get some money, I am going to buy Daddy a truck." You would have thought Daddy was Mr. Goodwrench. He was always fixing on something, cars, trucks, lawnmowers – it didn't matter. The earlier he got up, the more things he fixed. That's probably why those vehicles wouldn't run.

Daddy was also an early riser. He got up at the crack of dawn every day. He wanted Mama to get up when he got up so she could cook his breakfast. He loved either homemade biscuits and syrup or what he called flapjacks and scrambled eggs, which was his favorite. Mama, on the other hand, was not a morning person. She stayed up nearly all night cleaning or making us gets up to redo the cleaning if our cleaning didn't please her.

One morning Mama was upset with Daddy and she wouldn't get up so Daddy asked me to make his biscuits. I must have been eleven or so and didn't know how to make biscuits. I had seen Mama and Willie Ruth Make them. Willie Ruth was the ultimate biscuit maker. Her biscuits were a work of art. I tried to duplicate her skills. I made those biscuits with all that was within me. I put them in the oven and about forty five minutes later Daddy went to the oven and got the biscuits out. They must have weighed twenty pounds. I got Daddy a brown paper lunch bag, opened it and put two of my proudly made biscuits in it. I don't know if Daddy ate those biscuits, but if he did I know he was full. He never asked me to make him biscuits again.

Daddy worked his lawn service all spring and summer. As a matter of fact he was one of the first black men in Jackson to do yard work as an occupation. He did his work with pride. You would have thought he had a fleet of lawn service equipment but he took what he had and made the best out of it. He had bought a red 1945 Ford pickup truck. He painted it himself, and it displayed his Thompson's Lawn Service on the sides. Mama made fun of it but that that didn't bother him. He would said, "I'm not about form or fashion." He wasn't about buying new cars or trucks either.

Daddy had worked for a while and with Mama working part time too, they had earned enough money to move. He had already found a house. It was not far from where we lived. It was down Delta Drive which was part of Highway 49. Highway 49 North would take you all the way to the Mississippi Delta.

We Move to Carnation Street

We moved to Carnation Street. This was our third move and the third street that the name started with a "C". That seemed odd to me. I remember our address was 1034 Carnation Street which is locked in my head. I try to never forget where I came from. That way I can always see just how far I have come. It also helps me to know where I'm going. Delta Drive has since been renamed Medgar Evers Boulevard.

The house on Carnation Street had a living room and a dining room in which Mama did her bedroom combination design plan again to give the older girls a place to sleep. The house did have two bedrooms, but there was just one closet. The kitchen had no sink but there was a faucet in the back left corner of the room, where Mama put a table with a dish pan on it. The faucet only ran cold water so, we had to heat water on the stove to wash dishes or take a bath. We had to bathe in a tin tub, because our bathroom was on the back porch. It was a closet-sized room and there was not enough room for a tub. It was only large enough for a commode to fit in. So we were back to outdoor plumbing in a way. You had to sit sideways so your knees would not touch the wall.

The house had a fireplace in two rooms with gas space heaters in front of them. There were nice French doors separating the living room and dining room. But as I said, Mama had made the dining room into a bedroom. We ate in the kitchen. It was a little nicer than our Content Street apartment. There was more room and there were only three children per bed. No one was complaining.

We had a fairly nice backyard and it was fenced in. There were woods behind the backyard fence. The fence had bunches of honeysuckle hanging from it, that gave off the sweetest aroma. It was like living in the country rural, but in the city. Some people had chickens, and Daddy even had a hog that he had fattened up to slaughter. Our closest neighbor was a little elderly lady who lived in the house on the right side of us named Mrs. Mullins who was very odd. She would dash hot boiling water on the porch and yell as if a person was there.

On the other side was the "Garden of Eden" in which lived an elderly little man who asked us to call him Uncle Charley. He had a fruit tree orchard in his back yard with apple trees, pear trees, apricot trees, and plum trees. That was the best in the world. The first day we moved in Uncle Charley brought us bags of fruit to our house. He was a small framed, soft spoken man with fair skin and a little bend in his back that leaned him forward. Daddy and Mama thanked him for the fruit, and he smiled and turned and as he walked toward the door, Daddy asked him if he would like to have a cup of coffee. He said, "No thank you, maybe another time" and continued out the door.

We got settled in and things were going as well as Daddy expected. It was summer and he was still working, and that was good. As time passed we got to know some of the neighbors and their children. Mama still moved slowly on letting us associate with the children. She got us involved in cleaning, washing clothes, and making sure the house was kept clean and in order. On washday, which was Saturday, the older girls, that now included me, would line up one at a tin tub washing, two rinsing and one hanging clothes on the line. The tubs were sitting on a homemade wooden table that Daddy had made. We had a washboard that had a metal rippled center. It took nearly all day to wash and hang the clothes on the line.

I always prayed that the sun would shine, because if it was cloudy or cold it would take two days for the jeans to dry. They were hard to wring out and water would still be in them. If that happened we could not iron them on Saturday and there was no way you could iron on Sunday. Mama remembered the Sabbath and she kept it holy. We could do no work on Sunday. Thank God!

After we had been on Carnation Street for a few months Daddy and Mama started to have positive relationships with some of the neighbors. That was working out very well for us. Daddy met Mr. Lewis and Mr. Mims. Daddy and Mr. Lewis would take the elderly people on the street to pick up their commodities. That was USDA Government issued food. There was cheese, flour, yellow corn meal, butter, dried beans, canned peanut butter, dry skim milk, powdered eggs and canned meat. The food was issued once a month to elderly and low-income families.

Many elderly people couldn't stand in line long so Daddy would pick their food up for them. Now people get a food stamp card, can buy whatever food they desire and have the nerve to complain, God forbid. It's nothing wrong in getting food stamp assistance if an individual or families really need them. Sometimes when we are blessed we take the blessings for granted and have no sense of gratitude. As Paul put it whether I abound or abase I am content in the Lord.

Love Thy Neighbor

There were the Zachary's who lived a few doors down the street. We nicknamed Mrs. Zachary Sweetie Pie. She worked at the King Edward Hotel as a cook. She would send us bags of blueberry muffins so big one was a meal. People shared with each other back then. Whenever they gave her leftover food at work she always gave Mama some. I remember Mr. Zachary and daddy went hunting they brought back a big turtle, Mr. Zachary being a Grizzly Adams woodsy guy he was, made turtle soup and sent us some. To my surprise it had a very nice flavor somewhat like chicken.

All of the neighbors seemed to be nice people. The houses were not as close to each other as the houses on Content Street had been and the apartments were mostly on the end of the street. As Mama and Daddy got to know the neighbors they made their choice of those we could associate with, Mama started to let us play with the neighborhood children. I could play and visit with four girls in the neighborhood, Geraldine, Kavetta, Bessie Mae and Carol. We were all about the same age. When I went to Geraldine's we played cards or jacks and listened to 45 rpm rock 'n roll records on her record player. Willie Ruth and Rosa and my older brothers had also met some friends. Rosa's friend was Barbara who lived across the street and Willie Ruth's friend was Mary Alice. The boys and the older girls had a little more freedom than I did. They were able to go to house parties and ball games.

I had a pretty cool summer. Just being able to go play with someone other than a sibling for a little while was fun. Carol lived across the street but I could not go to her house so much because her mother was not home much. Geraldine lived several houses down the street and her mother was home all the time because she didn't work. The summer was winding down and it was almost time for school to start.

Most of our time on Carnation Street was hard times; we had some good memories however. Friendships were made and new experiences, mama had three ladies that she would associate with. She was still careful as to who she would associate with. She didn't take to people fast, she weighed ever relationship carefully. None of the ladies that mama associated with came to our house to visit, and I don't remember her visiting anybody either. Occasionally she would make a very short phone call to the ladies that she did talk with. She would only talk for a few minutes and that was it.

I do recall that our front door neighbor Mrs. Margaret Sterling had become ill. Mama had some flowers growing in the yard that she picked a lovely bouquet from; she put them in a jar that she wrapped in pretty paper and tied a bow at the top. She took the jar of flowers to the Sterling's front door and passed them to Miss Margaret's mother-in-law with the little card that said "get well soon love your neighbor." A short time after that Ms. Margaret sent mama a box filled with different kinds of Dinner Rolls, Danish and some fried chicken wrapped in wax paper, there was a little note inside the box that said thank you for the flowers, my husband had brought some of the food home that they gave him at work and he wanted us to share it with you, that's when we found out that Miss Margaret's husband was one of the cooks at the King Edward Hotel. Those King Edward Hotel workers were popping up all over the neighborhood. "Thank God."

Baby Makes Nine

Daddy and mama were happy again and you know it, Mama was having another baby. This time I kind of realized something was going on. I was excited because I was starting a new school and we were getting a new baby. The whole family was feeling good. Things were looking up.

When summer was over I started a new school – Mary Johnson Elementary down Delta Drive. We had to walk down the street and cross the highway to get to the school. I was in the fifth grade and hated it. My teacher was the same as the rest, and the children were not friendly at all. One boy in particular was so mean. One morning as I was walking to my desk he put his foot out to trip me. I kicked it out of my way and he stud up from his seat and punched me right in my stomach. It hurt so bad I thought I was going to die. When the teacher returned to the room the person who was taking names said I started it. The teacher didn't ask us anything. She just got out her belt and spanked us both. From that time on I resented her for her unfairness. I considered her another one of those teachers from you-know-where. I don't remember one good experience at that school. I was so glad when school was over that day. I found out that the bad boy who hit me was the brother of my oldest brother's friend Sammy Earl who lived around the corner on Oakley Avenue. My brother asked me if I wanted him to get him for me and I said no. After all, Sammy Earl couldn't help it if his brother was the seed of Satan.

Things were still alright. School was about over and spring was coming to an end. My grandmother was coming to stay with us for a while. I thought it was because Mama was having another baby and she wanted to be with Mama this time. Mama said every time she had a baby Mama Erna would come and care for her until she was on her feet again. I thought that was nice. Mama Erna wrote Mama a letter and told her that she would be in Jackson by the time school was out. She had been working for a nice white family in Leland who had two children and she didn't want to leave until the children were out of school. I was so excited because I had not seen Mama Erna since we left the Delta in 1952.

I remember that because the summer before we left the Delta Mama Erna gave me my first birthday party. The party was under the big pecan tree in her front yard. She baked cupcakes with white icing and sprinkles of all different colors and my cupcake had a candle on it. That was the first time I ever had cupcakes. We also had potato chips, hot dogs, Dixie ice cream cups and Kool Aid. It was also the first time I had ever seen a Pin the Tail on the Donkey game. I do remember that the party was a lot of fun. I was four years old and I can remember that like it was yesterday.

June came and school was out. Mama Erna was on her way. When she got here it was something to see. She arrived in a Dotty Cab with a big black trunk, a medium piece of luggage and a small overnight case. The luggage was cream colored and very nice. Mama Erna told Mama that the nice white lady she was working for gave it to her when she found out Mama Erna was coming to see about her daughter. At was a blessing that mama had a mother that cared so much about her. Just to take the time to come and care for her in a time of need. I know that when we were sick mama always nursed us back to health, with her and daddy's home remedies of teas, roots, rubs and tonics. Cod Liver Oil and Castrol Oil, yuck!! But we didn't have many doctor bills, that's for sure. On one or two occasions, I do remember when I had to go to the doctor; daddy and mama took me on Farish Street to Dr. Albert Britton's office, a black doctor downtown. Mama Erna was also famous for her use of Castrol Oil as a purging and cleaning of the body method.

I was so excited. It was as if a famous person was coming to our house. I was mama Erna's favorite grandchild, as my sisters and brothers would often say. But what they didn't realize was that I was the only grandchild that would stand as long as she needed, to oil her hair when she asked. God has no respect to persons, but He does have His Chosen People. Mama Erna had her chosen grandchild.

Heavenly Scent

When she got in the house and open the trunk, the top tray had all kinds of goodies in it. She had peppermint candy, long paper shelled pecans, and apples. You would have thought it was Christmas in June. I loved the overnight case she called the small case. When you opened it up there was a mirror at the top and inside there was wonderful smelling powder, Cashmere Bouquet Soap, and Evening in Paris perfume. She had the biggest hair comb I had ever seen and a can of Royal Crown Hair Grease. She had three of the prettiest lace and linen handkerchiefs in there too.

When Mama Erna got settled in, the fun started. She was young at heart and when we were watching American Bandstand on TV, Mama Erna got up and did the Twist with the Bandstand Dancers. My grandmother had many talents. She could sing, crochet doilies or scruffs that you could put on tables and tams, and going to church.

It was about a month before Mama Erna found work. She started working at the Independent Linen Company on Stonewall Street off of Bailey Avenue on one side and Mill Street on the other side. I found some paycheck stubs of hers from Independent Linen during that time and she had earned $1.16 for a week's work before taxes were taken out. She had earned the net sum of $.80 for the week. She would ride the bus to and from work. Mama Erna had lived in several big cities, traveling and cooking for white families, so getting around Jackson was no big deal. She was one hard working lady.

God Sent Us Angels In The Form of Good White Folks

One day when Mama Erna had gotten off work she came in and sat down, looked at me and said "**Tater,** get my comb and grease and come and scratch my head and oil my scalp." That was the first time I had answered to the nickname Tater, but that would not be the last time. I asked Mama why Mama Erna called me that and Mama said Mama Erna loved sweet potatoes and she loved to make sweet potato pone. I learned that to make sweet potato pone you grated the sweet potatoes rather than whip or mash them to make sweet potato pone. The different texture gave the sweet potatoes a different taste.

Mama Erna didn't work very long at Independent Lining, because standing on the concrete floor was bad on her feet. She was use to cooking or domestic work, more than that type of industry work. She just didn't like not being able to take a break and the long hours and little pay. One day she was on the bus coming home from work, a lady sat beside her and began to talk with her. The lady asked her where she worked and Mama Erna told her nowhere after today. The lady gave Mama Erna the telephone number of a lady who needed someone to work for her.

A few days later Mama Erna called the number to talk with the lady and she got the job. It was working for Mrs. Jane Cole a white lady who lived off Old Canton Road in northeast Jackson on Oakridge Drive. Mama Erna went to work for Mrs. Cole and liked it. She was back doing what she loved, cooking, but more cleaning and ironing. She worked three half-days a week. When Mama Erna couldn't go to work for Mrs. Cole, my sister Willie Ruth went in her place. Willie Ruth, as the rest of Mama's older girls, could cook and clean like full grown women. Mama had taught us well. She took pride in knowing that we knew how to conduct ourselves around all people. She always said good manners would carry you a long way, then she said always show respect and people will respect you.

We were taught to respect not only white people be adults of all races, older community members and people in authority. This teaching from our parents has served us well. "The Fear of the Lord is the Instruction of Wisdom and Before Honor is Humility" (Proverbs 15:33)

Sister, Sister

Rosa and Willie Ruth were good big sisters. Rosa was so grown up it seemed as if she were born that way. She was quiet, dignified, graceful and organized. Willie Ruth was precise, witty, dignified, more domestic, but just a tad rebellious. Both of my older sisters were very neat and clean. I know that they both made excellent grades in school. They had what seemed to be a lot of order in their lives. Rosa loved school and still does until this very day. I doubt if she ever made a grade under "A" in her early years in school. She and Willie Ruth were both high achievers, but it seemed as if Rosa was always in school. She thrived on it. I thought she was addicted or it could be that it just made her feel good. I don't know for sure.

    I don't remember Rosa and Willie Ruth ever having an argument. They got along so well and they both were very good to me. It was good for me to see the way they treated each other. It made me want to be a good big sister to Dorothy and Cecilia, my younger sisters as well as my younger brothers. I hoped they felt that I was just as good a big sister to them.

    Rosa was seventeen and getting ready to graduate from high school. She had gone to summer school two years so she could graduate early. That was also the year that my baby brother Lynn was born. Rosa's commencement was the first of August. I still remember that night as if it were yesterday. In the 50's, school graduations were held in the school's auditorium. When the music started the students walked in to Pomp and Circumstance and there was Rosa, head up, shoulders back, walking tall with a profound purpose. She had completed this goal. After a speech, the Principal and some teachers got up and called the graduates' names. When it was Rosa's turn she got up, standing with the grace of a five-star general, received her diploma with Honors and with the same grace returned to her seat.

Daddy and Mama were so proud. Daddy was just beaming. I hadn't seen him that happy in a long time. Rosa was very serious; I think she was born that way too. Sometime later Rosa told me that the night of graduation she had cardboard in her shoes to cover the big hole that was in her soles.

Rosa moved on to her job of working at Kolb's Cleaners on State Street. The most memorable thing about that job was that the arches in Rosa's feet fell, because she was standing on concrete all day at work and standing at beauty school long hours at night. Rosa was a hard worker and goal-driven. That has always been her way. She even supplemented her income sometimes doing domestic work.

Rosa and Mama Erna had that work thing down to a "T". It seemed as if they were working all the time. Mama Erna worked a few more months for Mrs. Cole and decided that she wanted to go back home to Leland. She recommended Mama to Mrs. Cole. She told Mrs. Cole that Mama could do everything that she could do and Mama was dependable. Mama was just who Mrs. Cole needed.

When mama called Mrs. Cole to inquire about the job, they talked for a little while. Mrs. Cole asked mama, how soon could she start to work? Mama told her "as soon as you want me to." Mrs. Cole told mama right away and before they got off the phone it was a done deal, mama was hired. My mother was so happy she got off the phone she started to shout, 'Thank You Lord," "Thank You Lord." Mama always knew when and how to get her shout on. I loved that about mama, she was not ashamed of praising God when He had done something good for her. Even in the hard times she knew to praise the Lord. I think that is why God kept on blessing her.

Christmas 1959

Mama started working for Mrs. Jane Cole in the fall of 1959 because Daddy's income just did pay the rent and utilities. When she came home with her daily pay, she would write a note for us to take to Hank's Grocery, which was just up the street across Delta Drive. When we took her note on Fridays which usually had a chicken, a bag of white potatoes, two cans of string beans, a loaf of bread, and some luncheon meat, and if she had enough money after we got the main items, a few packs of Kool-Aid for us and a six pack of Coca-Cola for her. Mama loved her Coca-Cola. The chicken would always be for Sunday dinner. Most of the time we just made lunch meat sandwiches during the week. We filled in with the government commodities that we received once a month.

As Mama continued to work for Mrs. Cole, I think she realized that Mama didn't have enough food for her children. After a while, Mrs. Cole would always send extra food home with Mama or something that Mama could use. When winter came, and Daddy's work was at a near standstill I think that Mrs. Cole realized also that Mama was not going to have very much for her family for Christmas.

When Mama got to work the Saturday before Christmas Mrs. Cole asked her "Rosie what do you want for Christmas?" Mama replied "Whatever God lays on your heart would be fine." She said

God Sent Us Angels In The Form of Good White Folks

Mrs. Cole left the house and when she came back she had all of these nice gifts for her and the children. Mama began to cry. Mrs. Cole said to her, "Rosie, don't cry, this is what Christmas is all about." Mama told her the night before she went to work that she had prayed and asked God to provide for her family for Christmas. All she said was "God I know that you will provide." She said that's why she began to cry. She knew that God had answered her prayer.

When Mrs. Cole brought Mama home, her car was packed with bags and boxes wrapped in Christmas paper. Mama got out of that car with a big smile on her face. She came to the door and asked us to go out to the car and get the boxes and bags. Boy! It was so much. There were food, clothing, and Christmas decorations. The bags that had the fruit in them had such a wonderful aroma. That Christmas Eve Mama was in the kitchen nearly all night. She cooked a big hen, dressing, potato salad, a chocolate cake, a coconut cake, and sweet potato pie. I was helper in the kitchen. I went to bed after everything was finished, but Mama was still up doing her finishing touches.

Christmas morning, when we woke up our house smelled of Christmas, a lot like my grandmother's trunk. Mama had put a fruit bowl on the coffee table. It held big red apples, navel oranges, peppermint candy, gum drops and mixed nuts. It was such a good feeling and Mama and Daddy were as happy as they could be. I thought to myself Mrs. Cole must be Santa Claus because all of those wonderful presents came from her. Mrs. Cole had a big heart and God surely did lay a lot on it.

I had a real doll house made out of metal and it had pretty little pink doll furniture. There was a doll family, a father, a mother, and two children. I also got a tea set, some toy aluminum cookware and a small baby doll. I just couldn't believe it. I had a real doll house. All I could think of was now I could put my shoeboxes away, the ones that held my paper dolls from the paper doll book and the ones that I cut out of the *Sears and Roebuck Catalog*. My sisters and brothers also had presents. There was something for everyone. Some of my older siblings had gotten roller skates and clothes, but the street where we lived wasn't paved so they had to go to the highway to skate.

That was one of the best Christmases our family ever had, the best one that I could remember since Daddy had worked at McCarty/Holman. Mama stretched those Christmas leftovers as far as she could. We had hen pie, hen sandwiches, and at the very end hen soup. As you can see, Mama was very creative. She was praying and hoping she could get more days to work.

We were truly blessed that God had place Mrs. Cole in our lives. I know that God always have a plan for His children that trust and believe in Him. He knew before my mother prayed what her needs were. He had already place in Mrs. Cole's heart to meet my mother's family needs. The only thing I know, as a child I watched the struggles my parents had but, they never gave up. They would keep holding on to their belief, that God would make it alright. When my mother told us that she had prayed I didn't know that she was planting a seed in me, that would remain in me all of my life. (Prayer truly changes things)

God had started a new work in our family's life, through the people He was preparing to place in my mother's life. As I played with my toys I had gotten for Christmas, I kept thinking about Mrs. Cole and how nice she was to do all that she had done for our family. Many times adults don't think about the impression that they make on children, but things that adults do and say can change the very course of child's life. I didn't just like Mrs. Cole because she gave us all those nice things for Christmas. I liked her because of the way she gave, the attitude that she had the joy that it seemed to give her, as she watched us take the things out of her car. The very smile that was on Mrs. Cole's face, the twinkle that was in her eyes knowing that she was doing what was right and good to help others.

I think what made Mrs. Cole's act of kindness so very unique was that doing that time, many whites had little concern about the welfare of black people. This in itself was a miracle; I know why

Mama kept praising God for what He had done for her family through Mrs. Cole. Mama indeed knew that all of those blessings came from God. God use people to carry out His ministries and missions to individuals and He indeed had a perfect missionary in Mrs. Cole.

The Maid's Grapevine

The maids in Jackson, as in many other areas in the south had a grapevine, so to speak. If the women were on the bus or in the neighborhood talking they told each other if they knew of a job opening at a white family's home in the city. They inquired around to see if someone they knew was interested in the job. Before my grandmother left Jackson, she took me visited our cousin Sylvia that lived on Bailey Avenue while we were there their cousin Ora who lived on Church Street called. Cousin Ora and their cousin, Mama Hattie who worked for the H. C. Bailey family, knew of a white lady looking for a cook. She asked Cousin Sylvia if she knew of any ladies in our family looking for work. Cousin Sylvia asked Mama Erna and she said "yes." Mama Erna told Cousin Sylvia, mama was looking for more work and she gave her our phone number.

New Year's Day came and went and my parents were still struggling. Those were very hard times. Cousin Ora called my mother about the white lady who needed someone to cook and gave mama the lady's phone number. Mama called and she got the job, working three days a week for Mrs. Vera Buford. The New Year seemed to be starting off well. Daddy wasn't pleased that Mama had to work more but he knew and he had no choice. He wasn't working much and he needed the help. So he gave in to Mama's working more.

Mama always got us off to school before she left for work and she tried to get home before we got home from school. She had something on cooking when we got home. Most of the time the meal would be beans, greens or peas, sweet potatoes, and cornbread sometimes it would just be buttermilk and cornbread. But it was good to come home to a meal. We made it through the winter and things seemed to be going alright for us. We had the basics – food, clothing and shelter and we were thankful.

When school was out for the summer, mama started letting me go to work with her. She would finish her work faster and she could get more done. The first time she took me to Mrs. Cole's house it had the appearance of an English cottage. When I went in, it was as if I was walking into the pages of *Better Homes and Gardens* magazine the house was so neat and clean, everything had a place. Mama asked me to dust, vacuum, and clean the bathrooms to my surprise, the house had two full bathrooms. When I finished dusting and vacuuming the living room and dining room, I started to clean the children's rooms.

Mrs. Cole had two children they were named Little Jane and Little Bill they each had their own room. That was the first time I had ever heard of the children in a family named the same as their mother and their father. Little Bill's room was neat as a pin. All of his clothes were hanging in his closet just as neat and orderly as could be. After I finished cleaning his room, I went to Little Jane's room and began cleaning. Her room didn't need much cleaning I just had to dust and vacuum it. She had a guitar and a set of drums in one corner of her room and her clothes hung neatly in her closet. I could only dream of having such a room.

At our house we had to hang our clothes on the back of the bedroom doors with big twenty-penny nails, because there was only one closet in our house. We had to re-press our clothes every time we got dressed because our clothes would get crushed hanging on that nail. As mama ironed all the Cole family's clothes, I would hang them in their closets.

While mama was working inside the house, Mrs. Cole spent most of her time outside in her backyard gardening. Her yard looked like a botanical garden. She had the most beautiful flowers, shrubbery and plants and everything was trimmed neatly with a wonderful precision. The flowers had such a beautiful aroma I could understand why she spent so much time out in her yard. She was in the yard for hours, humming songs, filling her birdfeeders with seed and putting water in the birdbaths. Mrs. Cole had compassion for all of God's creatures and God's people.

When Mama started working for Mrs. Buford, there was another lady named Ms. Luvenia already working there as the main maid. She had been working for Mrs. Buford for some time. She and mama got along well, as mama worked for Mrs. Buford longer she and Ms Luvenia became good friends. During the summer I would still worked for Mrs. Cole to earn money for things I needed. I really didn't mind because I only had to iron and do light cleaning.

Mrs. Cole was so clean that dusting and vacuuming was a breeze, but ironing was an all day thing. Mama and Mrs. Cole were a lot alike. They each kept their homes neat and clean and they both enjoyed sewing. Mrs. Cole made some of her clothes and her children's.

Mama said Mrs. Buford was a sophisticated socialite, different from Mrs. Cole, because Mrs. Cole was quiet and more domesticated. Mrs. Buford enjoyed having bridge parties, entertaining, and traveling the world. Mrs. Cole enjoyed more domestic activities such as decorating her home and gardening.

Mama enjoyed working for Mrs. Buford because they both loved to cook. Mrs. Buford fixed all kinds of wonderful decorative vegetable trays and fruit trays. She garnished dishes of all kinds, fruit and vegetable. One of Mrs. Buford's labored intense decorative things was making rosebuds out of red radishes or making parsley look like trees around platters. One of the best things Mama and Mrs. Buford ever made was chicken Tetrazzini. When Mrs. Buford entertained, whether it was her bridge club parties, or family dinners she always put her best foot forward. When she was getting ready for her bridge party she and mama were in the kitchen for hours, the day before getting all the food and serving dishes ready and set up. During that time I didn't see any of her children.

Mrs. Buford had all daughters. There was Ann, Jane, Bettye, Sissy, and Tot. Mama said Mrs. Buford was a good mother. She provided very well for her children. Her older daughters had their own family's homes and careers. When I started going there with Mama Sissy and Tot were the only children still at home. I didn't see Tot much because she was away at school most of the time.

Mrs. Buford told mama she had been a nurse at one time and she really liked nursing. After her husband died, with raising her children it was just better that she was home. The first time Mama took me to Mrs. Buford's house to help, I was again in one of those *Better Homes and Gardens Magazine* moments. But this time the house was a much larger two-story house on Carlisle Street in what is known as the Belhaven area of Jackson, because of the college with the same name in that part of town.

When mama and Mrs. Buford were in the kitchen preparing the food, I was doing light cleaning and making sure that the house was in order. After I got through dusting and vacuuming downstairs, I would go upstairs to clean and make beds. I really didn't have much to do because Ms Luvenia would have done some of the cleaning. By the time I was through with making beds upstairs it would be time for the lunch. Mama had made me a sandwich and on the side of the plate she put some little cookies. I had never tasted anything like them. Later I saw the bag of cookies on the counter in the kitchen. The name of the cookie was *Danish Wedding Cookies*. I love them to this very day.

I had lunch on what Mama called the sun porch. It was on the back of the house and screened in. The Buford's had a little brown dog named Ginger. Ginger was what we called a wiener dog. She was a tad overweight and carefree dachshund. That was the day I saw Mrs. Buford's youngest daughter Sissy for the first time. She came in through the back and started to talk to Ginger. Mama came to the door and introduced Sissy to me. Sissy had blonde hair, all bouncing and behaving and she had the most beautiful wide smile you could ever imagine. Her eyes twinkled as if she had seen something she had never seen before. She looked at me and just smiled and said "Hi". She didn't stay long and I didn't see her any more that day.

Mama was doing the laundry while I was sitting on the sun porch. She bought me a large basket of clothes and she asked me to fold them. She said after you finish with the clothes and sweep I will be finished for the day. Then she had me to sweep the sun porch. After that all of her work was done it was time for us to go home. Mama had already call daddy to pick her up, and just as she was coming out of the back door daddy drove up.

When every daddy would come up the drive way he would always check to see if Mr. Charley was about. Mr. Charley was Mrs. Buford's handy man. Daddy didn't take to men looking at mama and I could see why. My mother had a very nice figure in large shapely legs. Her clothes fit well on her slim body. Mama had put on a little weight but her clothes still fit nice and neat, and she was always clean as could be. Her clothes were never too tightly clinging to her body. She kept her hair neat as well. Just the way she taught us to groom ourselves. If Mr. Charlie was around daddy acted like he was in such a big hurry. As if he had something very important to do sometimes he would hunk his horn excessively, which you know got on mama's nerve. You could always tell if mama was upset with daddy she would get in the truck rolled her eyes and tighten her lips. Sometimes to aggravate mama more if she acted mad daddy would speed out of the driveway. She would just look over at him and ask him, "why are you acting like such a heathen?" he would just put this little smirk of a smile on his face slow down a bit and just keep driving. I thought that was to show mama he was in charge.

Mama called those actions of daddy's, his nut moments. When she would get out of the truck she would just look at him and say, "You're such a nut." Daddy would say something smart like "yeah but I'm your nut," and mama would just laugh and say "I must be a nut too," and they both would laugh. At that point it seemed that all was well. One thing I remember about my parent is they never stayed angry with each other for long periods of time and they really talk to each other all the time.

The Teen Years

By the time I was fourteen, I had my first summer job working for Mrs. Cole. I worked two days a week and earned $4.00, a day which was big money to me. I was really learning to work well. I could starch and iron Mr. Cole's and Little Bill's shirts as well as Mama and I was pretty good at cleaning too. Sometimes when Mrs. Cole didn't feel like taking me home she would ask Little Bill to take me. She had nicknamed him Bubba. Mrs. Cole was a petite lady with a long slurring southern drawl, I hung on every word. That was really a joy ride, because Bubba had this neat 1957 canary yellow Thunderbird convertible. You can only imagine how I felt back then, riding in such a beautiful car.

    Not one word passed between us as we drove, but in my mind, as the wind blew warm on my face, I would imagine that I was on my way to a far off place where the palm trees swayed in the wind and the ocean water was so blue that it glowed in the light of the sun, much like those beaches in the Beach Boys, or Annette and Frankie Avalon moves we used to watch on television or in the movie theaters in the late fifties and sixties.

    While I worked for Mrs. Cole that summer, I only saw Little Jane maybe four times. She was a quiet girl. Her room was a cozy place with a warm feel to it. I could only dream of how it would be to have a room of my own. As life dictated as a child I never did have my own room. Sometimes when I was cleaning Little Jane's room I would imagine it was my room. I would clean her room longer that way I would have a longer time to pretend. I just couldn't get those nice closets in their rooms out of my mind.★ All of their clothes fit in so neatly and when you ironed the clothes they stayed pressed.

At our house we would iron our school clothes for the week but they had to be re-ironed because they would get wrinkled from being mashed together because our closets were homemade. Talking about double work! I just didn't see the point to all the ironing over and over. Nobody said anything; we just did as we were told. Our parents didn't take suggestions from children in those days. Children were to be seen and not heard. That was a common belief and that is just what we were – seen but not heard.

We had to walk what our parents called the chalk line. That meant that we had boundaries that we just didn't cross. Parents demanded respect and obedience from their children. From generation to generation those boundaries has been diluted to near zero, it is a shame to say.

I always wondered what was it that made people know the punishment for disobeying, but they would disobey any way. We just thought it was natural to obey your parents. However, there were several occasions that one of their children would step outside of their boundaries. We were quickly chastened, and brought to remember that mama and daddy were in charge. Hence the Bible saying *"spare the rod spoil the child"* was adhered to religiously. Today it would be called child abuse.

Summer's End

My work that summer turned out to be very beneficial. Not only did I get to earn some money, but I got some socializing in. I had made a few friends among the neighborhood children. During the 60's there were not many places black children could go to have social interaction. We made our own fun, mostly by going to backyard parties. We called those parties Friday or Saturday night fish fry's or wiener roasts. The parties were at a neighbor's house and we were always chaperoned by the parents, of the children's house that we visited. We never had the weekend parties at our house, because Mama was very conservative. She didn't want all that sinning around her. You know, all that listening to boogie-woogie music and dancing as she called it, so she would just let us go sin at someone else's house.

If my two older sisters were invited to a party Mama wanted me to go too. I think it was because she knew she could trust me to tell her if anyone there was acting ugly. I knew that if I got to telling too much, my sisters wouldn't want me around so I was just like those three little monkeys. I didn't hear nothing, I didn't see nothing and I didn't say nothing and I kept on going to those parties. When I went to the parties I just sat and watched the older children dance, so I could learn the latest dance steps and we all watched American Bandstand. I guess the combination of going to the yard parties and watching Bandstand helped me learn most of the latest dance steps faster. Everyone would have such a good time. There was only one what you would call "a bad girl" in the group. That was Barbara who was a real show-off. She was the first girl I ever saw do what you would call "dirty dancing" and I mean that literally. There was also Teeny Bit who was the sister of Willie Ruth's friend Mary's sister. Teeny Bit could make her whole body shake just like a bowl of Jell-o. While dancing to any rock 'n roll record she just stopped and her body wiggled like Jell-o to the music. That was something to see.

The summer proved to be a real learning experience for me. I had met new friends when I went to yard parties. A little dancing with some of the neighborhood boys made me feel a little better about myself. Surely junior high would be better than elementary school. I was getting ready to start at Lanier Junior/Senior School. Black children had to walk to school and Lanier was about three miles each way from our house. Children back then got plenty of exercise. Coupled with having to carry those heavy books, we were in very good shape. We didn't have fast food restaurants in our neighborhoods; therefore we didn't have much childhood obesity. It was no big deal because everyone had to walk to school with the exception of a few children whose parents dropped them off. Everyone left home about the same time so you had lots of company on the way to school.

I did notice that most of the homes were very nice. I knew that black people lived on Whitfield Mills Road. I asked my sister about the houses. She told me that many of the doctors, teachers, preachers, lawyers and other professional black people lived in that area. There were two long beautiful light-colored brick homes side by side up on the hill and other very large homes. She told me those homes belong to the Bank's family, a prominent black family of lawyers. There were also very nice homes on Maple Street, the street that Lanier School was on.

WOKJ radio stations DJ Joby Martin always played "Hit the Road Jack" by Ray Charles when it was time to leave home. My older sisters would have the radio on, and they told mama the reason was, so that we wouldn't to be late for school, as if we didn't have a clock. Mama was alright with their explanation, as long as we were going to school.

Lanier Dear

When school started in 1962 I was ready for my new adventure. It was altogether different. We had to change classes for each subject and you got to pick an elective class. That was a fun class of your choice. Maybe, just maybe, with more than one teacher all day, I stood a fighting chance. I was doing well in the seventh grade and then it happened. I encountered Mrs. Sadie McGee, my physical education teacher from the bottomless pit. The army would have loved to have one drill sergeant with her capabilities. She would make you drop and do 50 pushups if you just breathed loud and that took place after you just finished 100 jumping jacks. I was in her class two days a week. I never saw her in a dress but her PE uniform was so white that it was almost blinding the white pants, white shirt, white KEDs and socks. She was one clean lady.

God must have known that I needed something to balance those mad-with-the-world personalities, that some of my teachers had. He sent a miracle working teacher named Mrs. A. K. Lattimore. She actually made mathematics seem easy. Sometimes she would ask me if I wanted to stay after school and she would help me with problems, I was having difficulty with. I would say "Yes, ma'am."

She would take time to show me the functions of the problem and how to work with abstracts and formulas. She gave me a times table sheet and the math formulas for algebra to study. She really helped me a lot. I was so happy because she didn't judge me because I didn't know how to do the problems. She made me feel at ease. I think that is what made me able to do the work. I will never forget what Mrs. Lattimore did for me. Daddy and Mama were really big on education. They wanted us to make something of ourselves. Daddy said education is the key to everything. He wanted us to do well in our class work. That is just what Mrs. A.K. Lattimore did; she made sure that I did well in math.

The Movement

In 1962 there was a lot going on with the Civil Rights Movement. Everyone was on pins and needles. Voter registration for black people and James Meredith integrating the University of Mississippi did, in fact, have Mississippi burning. But there was unrest nationwide, from the east coast to the west coast and all states in between. There were race riots in Cambridge Massachusetts and, New York, Cairo, Illinois and Los Angeles, California. The KKK was, and is, in every state of the Union. Many of the Klansmen came from the north, the east coast and the west to do war at Ole Miss up in Oxford. This was because a black man was trying to enroll in school there. It didn't matter that he had been in the Air Force for nine years and that he had fought for his state and country.

They numbered in the hundreds and thousands. Hate has no boundaries. When you are taught to hate for any reason, it is a sin against God. It was bad in every county in Mississippi north to south, east to west. Black people were being burned out, hunted like animals and many times our law enforcement was in the pack with the sheets over their heads. Many white women were in the White Citizen's Council and the KKK in league with their husbands and they made their hired help's lives a living hell. However, there were many white people who had enough God in them to do the right thing for the black people who worked for them.

My sister Willie Ruth joined the NAACP her senior year at Lanier. She, along with a large group of freedom marchers consisting of students from all the black high schools and colleges, Jim Hill, Brinkley, Tougaloo, Jackson State and some white clergy and other whites were marching from Lanier to down town Jackson. When they got to Capital Street on their way to the Capitol Building, they were lining one side of the street. There they were met with a force from hell.

The Jackson Police, Mississippi Highway Patrol and Hinds County Sheriff's Department met them with fire hoses and German Sheppard dogs. Willie Ruth and all the marchers who couldn't get away were put in paddy wagons and carried to the stockyard on the Jackson fairgrounds. They were placed in a pen with animal dung (animal waste) covering the ground.

When Daddy and Mama got the call that Willie Ruth had been arrested Mama almost fainted. She started saying, "Lord have mercy, and Lord have mercy." Daddy told her, "Rosella, just calm down." He had done some work for Officer Skinner, a Jackson policeman and they had a good relationship. Daddy called him and he met Daddy at the fairgrounds the next morning. They got Willie Ruth out and when she got to Daddy she really smelled terrible. Mama was so happy Willie Ruth was alright that all she could say was "Thank you, Lord" over and over.

Daddy told Willie Ruth that he was proud of her, but he had no choice but to forbid her from marching any more. She told him "yes sir" but I could tell she didn't want to. Later I asked her how she felt. She had a big bruise on her leg. I asked her about it and she said it was from where the force of the water from the fire hose slammed her against a brick wall. She said that the water burned like fire. I had so many questions but I could tell she was tired so I let her rest. I was proud of her too.

She didn't march again but she started going to church a lot. I found out that she was still working for voter registration with the NAACP. I knew Daddy and Mama knew that she wasn't going to church just to see Jesus. They just acted as if they believed she was going to church because she loved the Lord so much. When Willie Ruth graduated that year, she and Rosa left a legacy for my brother William Joseph and me to follow. They both left of good report, as the Bible says and a reputation for being academically smart.

Good Men Dying

Just at a time when things were going so well with classes that eighth-grade year, tragedy struck again. It was November 22, 1963 and we had just come from lunch. Our class was in the library when the news flash came on the television and the announcer said President John F. Kennedy had just been shot in Dallas, Texas while riding in a motorcade. It seemed as if my heart stopped for a moment. A short time later the same announcer came on and said it was official. President Kennedy had been pronounced dead. All I could think about was his wife and children, and I began to cry. I cried a long time, until I had no more tears. Classes were cancelled the rest of that day, which was one of the saddest days in my life.

It seemed as if good men were dying every few months. It had only been six months since the murder of Medgar Evers in the front yard of his home. June 12, 1963 was the first saddest day I had known. His wife and children had this awful tragedy to happen at their home. I couldn't imagine. We lived not very far from where that shooting happened. It seemed as if peace would never come to this state, and now our whole nation was in complete unrest with war and death all around us in America and in Vietnam.

Our nation carried on with the new president. School and life went on as usual. All of us still had a lot of work to do. There was a lot going on with the civil rights movement. There were marches, sit-ins, speeches and protest after protest. There was a lot of killing, singing and college campus unrest.

With all of that going on, there were still some people, white, black, Jews and Gentiles, working together to try to make this state and country a better place for everybody to live. Mississippi certainly had its share of racial strife, but there were still some people in the background who were trying to give a helping hand to those who were treated unjustly.

Not to downplay the civil rights movement, or the advances that were made by those who worked so hard and those who gave their very lives for equal rights and fair treatment, for blacks and others. I just know that in the midst of all that was going on there were white people in Mississippi who just did what was right in their hearts for the black people who were part of their lives.

Such were the white people who my mother worked for. Who became a part of her family and allowed her to become a very special part of their families out of love and respect. I know I would not have been afforded some of the nicer things in life that I had if it had not been for Mama's "Good White Folks Angels."

As I look back at and think about the people who stirred up racial hate and even some today. I still wonder why they cannot get the hate out of their heart. But I guess it's not for me to understand the haters. I have to dwell on what is positive and remember all of the good white people that superseded the hatemonger. because only what you do for God matters. And God commands us to forgive.

I had many emotions, as the year passed so many lives changing experiences, a young girl trying to survive and understand all of the things that were going on around me. The actions of people the news reports, trying to learn where my place was in society, as a member of our family, and just trying to learn how to live and exist in such a confusing world. Trying to live up to my mother and father's expectation there was truly a lot on my mind. And I know there was a lot on my mother and father's minds also.

On August 4, 1964 three Civil Rights worker James E. Chaney, Andrew Goodman, and Michael Swherner, all in their early twenties were killed in Philadelphia, Mississippi up in the Mississippi Delta. They were working with voter registration more senseless killing. If all the killing from the pass had not stop people from marching and fighting for freedom. What made the sin sick people doing the killing think that more killing was the answer they had to be demon possessed. They were killing white folks, black folks anyone that did not agree with their hate. I often wondered what made these people think that God or Jesus would think it was alright to burn something as sacred as the Cross that Jesus died on, where his precious blood was shed to save us from our sins. I know beyond the shadow of a doubt that that is blatant blasphemy and the highest level of disrespect of God, Jesus and the Holy Ghost. It was surly going to take God to change the hearts and minds of these people everywhere. It was time for me to get my mind on school, so I just stopped watching the news on television; I was going with out of sight out of mind.

School started in September, and I was placed in some of the best teachers rooms. I could tell that this was going to be a very good school year. With so much unrest all around us it was nice to have some sense of peace. If only for a little while concentrating on class work would be much better than thinking of all the violence around us.

Mama was having a hard time, because she had to leave Lynn my baby brother at a little day care she had found, but she had to work. Sometimes when money was tight she would take Lynn to work with her. Mrs. Buford didn't seem to mine, and it helped mama so much. If Mrs. Buford handy man Mr. Charley was around her house cleaning the yard. I think daddy was a bit jealous so mama would also take Lynn to work with her so daddy would not act up.

Sissy told me once when we were talking that she remembered on one occasion that daddy had come to pick Mama up for work, she said she heard daddy talking rough to mama. Sissy said she ran out of the back door went up to daddy's truck; stood at window looked him and eyes and said "don't you talk to my Roe, Roe like that." She said daddy just looked at her and screeched his eyes at her.

I told Sissy that she sure was brave, I would never have the nerve to approach daddy like they. I knew from that Sissy sure did love mama a lot. I know what Sissy was talking about. Daddy did have a bad temper at times and a very short fuse from at times. Most of the time when he would get upset and act up, Mama would ignore him. We had so many memories, some good and some not so good but all and all the good out weighted the bad. As the time passed it seemed as if the school year was going so fast. We were in the last quarter of the school year.

Like a Princess

We were getting ready for the Freshman/Sophomore Ball. During that time Mrs. Buford was giving me all of Sissy's clothes. When she bought a new wardrobe for Sissy, I got her old one, so I always had very nice clothes to wear. Mama had told Mrs. Buford about me going to the Ball and Mrs. Buford sent me the most beautiful multi-colored pastel after-five dress with a beautiful wide white petticoat. I was going to be escorted by Ronald Lattimore, he was a tall very good looking fellow. I was only fourteen and while I didn't really date at that age, Mama and Daddy let me go with Ronald because he was a very nice young man.

Mama knew that his mother taught at Lanier and she was ok with a person if she knew their parents. The night of the Ball, when I got dressed I felt like a fairy princess. When Ronald arrived he had gotten me a beautiful wrist corsage that matched my dress. Willie Ruth had fixed my hair in a beautiful French Roll in the back with Shirley Temple curl bangs. You could tell that Mama was really proud of the way I looked and we had Sissy and Mrs. Buford to thank for it.

Ronald's father drove us to the school. The gym was decorated beautifully but there were wall-to-wall chaperones. The music was playing, and the DJ had on the latest records. Sam Cook was singing "Darling You Send Me" and after that we danced to Mickey's

Monkey. Going to those neighborhood wiener roasts was really paying off. I was dancing all over the place and I loved it. Ronald seemed to be having a nice time also and he was a very good dancer. We both had a fun night. At the end of the dance the DJs would always play "Good Night Sweetheart, It's Time to go". The dance ended our school year, and it was almost summer again.

Mama had started working full time for Mrs. Cole, because Mrs. Cole had surgery and Mama knew Mrs. Cole needed her more. Since school was out, Mama said I could help Mrs. Buford. Sissy was gone for the summer and Mrs. Buford wanted someone to clean the house on the weekends. I worked for her on Saturdays.

Most Saturday morning's Mrs. Buford wanted to have breakfast in bed. Her favorite breakfast was a poached egg, half a pink grapefruit with sections separated, one strip of lean bacon, fried golden brown, a slice of dry toast cut in triangles, a cup of black coffee and orange juice.

Mrs. Buford still wanted Mama to work at least one day a week. I think she didn't want Mama to leave her to work full time for someone else. I worked for Mrs. Buford the whole summer. Her daughter Ann was married to Mr. Eugene Yelverton Jr. (Gene) Mrs. Buford loved to have Sunday dinners for her family. Her son-in-law, her daughters and friends would be there.

Her son-in-law loved to cook and Mrs. Buford let him. Most of the time when she had the Sunday dinners, she wanted Mama there to help with the cooking. She and Mr. Gene thought no one could make cornbread or candied yams like Mama. I would help wash the dishes. After dinner was served, Mr. Gene always told Mama, "Rosa, be sure you all eat before you leave and take the rest with you." I thought that was so nice of him. When Daddy picked us up we had lots of bags. Mama stretched that food so it would last nearly all week. That helped a lot because Daddy's work was still slow. He had only gotten two new yards all summer. The lady who lived in front of Mrs. Cole and another neighbor were letting him do their yards. My older brothers helped him as he got more work.

I am sure that Mrs. Cole had something to do with daddy's getting those yards. Knowing the hard times mama was having. It was just in Mrs. Cole nature to try to help in any way she could. Mrs. Cole and daddy were very distant to say the least; he still had a lot of hostility, because of some of the injustices that had happened personally to him. I know that Mrs. Cole helped him because of her love for mama and that was still good. What happened here was part of God's divine plan.

Sissy's Return

When Sissy came home from vacation she had a beautiful tan she was almost brown as me and her hair seemed blonder. She was in real good spirits. That morning when I got to work, I served Mrs. Buford breakfast as usual. I began to do my work. I washed all the dishes and just as I was almost finished with everything, Sissy came downstairs. She looked at me and she said, "Clementine, can you dance? There is this dance I've been trying to learn. Do you think you could teach me? The name of the dance is the Watusi." When we went up to Sissy's room she had every rock 'n roll record in the world. Sissy didn't discriminate, black artist, white artist, everybody, she had them all from Elvis to Chubby Checker. We did the Watusi the rest of the day. And to my surprise she was really getting the steps. She was a white girl with rhythm.

The summer went really well. I tuned fifteen that July and I enjoyed going to work even more now, especially when Sissy was home. We would get in as much dancing as possible. Mrs. Cole was doing better and Mama was back at Mrs. Buford's more days and also working for the Yelvertons. One day I overheard Mrs. Buford telling Mama about Sissy's and my dancing and they were both laughing. They thought it was cute. I was glad Mrs. Buford wasn't upset because she was paying me half of the time to dance with Sissy.

Sissy reminded me of the character Annie Potts played in the television series "Any Day Now", Mary Elizabeth, (ME) the white girl who was friend of the black girl in the late fifties and sixties. They had many life changing experiences together and grew up to remain very close friends. Sissy and I were friends, she was truly a free spirit and her room sometimes looked like a whirlwind had hit it, clothes tossed across the swinging door, shoes on the floor, closet in disarray. I simply loved being around Sissy she had such energy, she was bubbly and happy all the time.

I had just finished cleaning Sissy's room, when she closed the door and started asking me questions about school, boys and all the latest dance steps. We talked a while about our likes and dislikes. To my surprise, there was not much difference in the things that we liked and disliked. We were just two teenage girls having a good time. In the midst of the race riots, protests, marches, and the singing "We Shall Overcome". Sissy and I had overcome and didn't even know it.

Sissy & Catherine

The Metallic Bouffant Dress

Her smile was etched in my mind and she had a heart of gold. I remembered this incident that happened between Sissy and her mother. Sissy wanted to give me a beautiful metallic bouffant dress. Mrs. Buford explained to Sissy that she had just bought the dress, and Sissy had only worn the dress once and she could give it to me at a later time. Sissy yelled in a loud voice "No mother, I want to give it to her now." I felt so badly for Mrs. Buford. As they tugged on the dress, it ripped.

That was an awkward moment for me. I felt badly for Sissy too because she wanted to do something sweet for me, but her mom was right. A few weeks later, Mrs. Buford sent the dress to me. It was a long time before I wore the dress. I felt that I was the reason the incident happened.

When I went back to work all was well, it was as if nothing had happened. I worked the rest of the summer and Sissy caught up on all the latest dances. She learned to stroll and, to do the Boston Stomp and we both cut our hair into Beatles hairstyles. I'll bet we walked to New Orleans with Fats Domino a thousand miles, we had a fun summer. I did pretty good working, I was able to buy all my own school supplies. I felt that helped daddy and mama a lot, the less they had to buy. God showed me so much favor in my friendship with Sissy. She was one of the reasons that many of my insecurities were overcome. I was very proud of the fact that she treated me as if I was just a regular friend. We didn't just groove on a Sunday after-noon we grooved every opportunity we got. She was such a fun loving girl, carefree and bubbly all of the time just fun to be around.

I think the whole world would be better if people somehow could become color blind to skin color, unaware of race, religion, nationality, or any other factors that could cause discrimination, bigotry, and hatred. Of course God did give us a kind of **love** that fits that description it is called **Agape Love.**

As I think back to age twelve when I confessed my belief in Jesus and was baptized I knew a change took place in me. However, I didn't know much about the Holy Spirit because not much was taught on the third person of the Trinity. I didn't know what had happened, but I did feel different. I knew as a little child that there was a force much greater than anything or anyone that was in my life to help me.

I looked at my mother and father and the faith that they had, no matter how hard life situations got, they held on knowing that a change was going come. So we all knew that something much greater, a force if you will was sustaining us all. It had to be the love of God that gave them the strength to persevere.

"The Greatest Need in the World Today Is Love, More Love for Each Other and More Love for God Above!" (Helen Steiner Rice)

Know therefore that the Lord thy God, he is God, the faithful God, which kept covenant and mercy with them that love him and keep his commandments to a thousand generations. (Taken from The Bible Promise Book for Women: By Barbour Publishing Inc. King James Version)

**Picture of Mama's
Good White Folks Angels
Miss Ann's Wedding Day**

Babies and More Babies

As I was starting the ninth grade, my older sister Rosa married in 1962, she and her husband was getting ready to start their family, and they were having their first child. She had married a school teacher, Lee A. Garner, who Mama and Daddy were very proud of daddy loved him like a son. Mama and daddy were getting ready to have their first grandchild. Mama thought it best that Lee and Rosa stay with us until the baby was born. Since it would be easier for her to help take care of Rosa, I thought that was a good idea also, because all of us loved my brother-in-law. He had the most beautiful smile and very intelligent. We were all so excited about the new baby coming.

Mom was back working for Mrs. Buford and still worked for Mrs. Cole. This was working out very well because she didn't have to stop working for either of the ladies whom she had grown to love so much. Mrs. Buford's daughter, Miss Tot had married in 1964 and she and Mr. Bill Bailey were the proud parents of twin girls. Mama would go to help Miss Tot from time to time and I got to do some babysitting for her. Mama had work all the time now and things were getting better.

Mama was spending a lot of time at Mrs. Tot Bailey's because Mrs. Buford had gone on one of her famous overseas trips. Mrs. Buford wanted Mama to spend a little time at her house while she was gone, so she could cook and help care for Sissy. During that same time Mama and Miss Tot were cooking and building a close relationship. They just had good times together mama loved working for her because, Miss Tot bragged about Mama's cooking and how much Mama was teaching her. That made Mama feel appreciated Miss Tot was so proud when mama taught her how to string and cook Kentucky Wonder Green Beans and how to make corn pudding and homemade pickles. Tot said Mama was like a mother to her.

Everything was coming together. With Mama and Daddy both working, we were doing okay. They both seemed happy and less stressed. It seemed as if Daddy was getting more yard work and steady pay checks and with Mama working more for Mrs. Bailey, Mrs. Buford, and Mrs. Cole, she was working full time.

Life's Training Lessons

Mama took all her younger daughters to work with her and she trained us how to work. She said an honest day's work was better than stealing or no work at all. There was no shame in making an honest living. She insisted that it was not what you did that made the person but how you did it. She also said there was nothing like a good education. She spoke a lot about how she wished she had finished school. Mama could read, write, spell extremely well and count. That's about what you learned in school in her day. I think she did well with the education she had. She knew how to teach her children the difference between right and wrong.

My mother was letting us know that she was not ashamed of being a maid because she did her work well. She wanted us to see how other people lived and she wanted us to know that if we worked hard enough we could live better. She was giving us an education in life so we had an understanding of social graces and work ethics, which were very important to her.

She often cautions us on the type of people to associate with. In some ways I thought my mother was prejudice but later in life I learned that she was training us really on a Bible principle. When Moses led the children of Israel out of Egypt and out of the wilderness to the Promised Land, when he was turning the leadership over to Joshua he warned Joshua not to let the children of Israel even associate with the other tribes in that area. Moses warning to the children of Israel was done to let them know not to carry on the practices of the heathen nations around them and worshiping idols and acting as a heathen. Case in point my mother did not want us to act like heathens.

The Girdle Incident

Mrs. Buford really believed in girdles. As a matter of fact, the only falling out that I remember Mama telling me about between the two of them was the time Mrs. Buford needed help with her girdle. She had taken a bath, and her body was still damp. Mrs. Buford wanted Mama to help her pull her drawstring corset up on her body. As they struggled to get the corset up, it refused to come. Mama said they pulled and they pulled but it just wouldn't budge.

Mama said Mrs. Buford said "**Pull harder** Rosie". Mama said, "I am pulling!" Then it happened the last time Mrs. Buford yelled "Pull!" Mama said "Oh, foot". She turned and stormed out of the room, went downstairs, got her purse, called Daddy to pick her up and headed out the door walking. Mama said she had gotten to the corner of Woodrow Wilson and State Street when she saw Daddy at the light. Mama didn't say a word all the way home. From Mrs. Buford's house on Carlisle Street to Woodrow Wilson is about five miles so you can see Mama had made good time. I'm sure the fact that she was angry made a difference in how fast she got to that intersection.

Mama stayed home about two weeks. Mrs. Buford called Mama crying, "Rosie, why are you doing me like this?" Mama began to explain to Mrs. Buford that she had arthritis really bad in her hands and she had tried the best she could to help her with her girdle. They both laughed and Mrs. Buford said, "Rosie you know I love you."

Mama said "you know I love you, too" and she said all was forgiven. When Mama went back to work, Mrs. Buford had a beautiful gift set of Estée Lauder Youth Dew perfume for her. After that incident, Mama and Mrs. Buford's relationship seemed to grow stronger. I think Mrs. Buford had a deeper respect for Mama after that. From that time on if Mrs. Buford had any family problem she would always confide in Mama.

The week Mama went back to work for Mrs. Buford, after she had served dinner Mama noticed Mrs. Buford had had one too many cocktails, She told Mrs. Buford "I am going to call my ride now." Mrs. Buford insisted on taking Mama home. Not wanting to cause confusion Mama said "Yes ma'am." Mama said her heart was beating so fast she thought she was going to faint. She was scared to death. She said by the time they got to the end of State Street, the police pulled them over.

The officer got out of his car and came over to the window of Mrs. Buford's car. He said "Ma'am, did you know you were speeding?" Mama said Mrs. Buford looked him dead in the eyes and said, "Yes sir, I am sorry but my maid is sick and I was trying to get her home." Mama said she wasn't laying sweat beads were falling down her face, and she was shacking like a leaf. She must have looked sick to him, because he let them go. Mrs. Buford told Mama not to tell anyone about what happened. And Mama kept her secret until 2005 when she told me what happened.

The year was passing so quickly it seemed as though time had speeded up. The summer wasn't easy with cotton growing. Mama was good looking but Daddy sure wasn't rich, as the song said. Times were still hard. Mama started having back problems. She went to a doctor with whom Mrs. Buford arranged an appointment for her. The doctor told Mama she had a slipped disc in her back. Because of arthritis, Mama was in a lot of pain. She was put on bed rest with pain medicine.

Sometimes mama's pain was so bad until she couldn't sleep. Daddy being the home remedy Doctor he was, made mama a tardy to see if it would help her to sleep. Of course the tardy was made with Jack Daniels. It was only about two tablespoon full; keep in mind mama had never had a drink of alcohol in her life. Now that alcohol coupled with the pain reliever that the doctor had prescribed had a bad effect on mama. I don't know if she was having a bad dream or hallucinating but she awakened screaming as loud as she could. It scared us so bad that all us were just looking and shaking. We just didn't know what to do. Daddy however knew just the right thing to do. He went in the kitchen made pot of coffee and brought mama a cup, he told her to sip it slowly. I guess he knew she was stoned out of her head. Well daddy got mama calmed down and she finally got to sleep. She awakened the next morning with a headache, she took her every faithful BC powder and drank a Coca-Cola and in a while she was all better. After that incident mama never let Daddy's doctor on her again. I guess daddies tardy was just too strong for mama especially with her being on pain relievers, it was just not a good mix.

Mama stayed in bed for about three weeks, and gradually got to stirring around again. She seemed to be getting a little better, but she was still moving sort of slow. The heating pad that she laid on seemed to give her some comfort, we were glad to see mama doing better. She had suffered so; by the time she went back to the doctor her pain was almost completely gone. The doctor still wanted her to take it easy a bit longer just to make sure she wouldn't have a relapse.

Mama went back to work but she only worked half days. When she was at work she would take breaks in between work task to keep her back from hurting. The short work day helped and when she came home she would lie down and rest. The older children would take care of the cooking and cleaning at our house. We knew we had to let mama rest so she could get well. Everyone kept asking mama how her back was filling. She said that it felt better each day, we were all happy to hear that.

Back to Leland

Just at the time mama was feeling better a letter came from my aunt in Leland. The letter said that Mama Erna had a fall. She had broken her hip but that wasn't the worst news. The doctors had found that she had liver cancer and it didn't look good. They had given her six months to live. Mama began to scream. It scared us so bad, I began to tremble. When we rushed in to see what the matter was, she was just saying "Oh no, oh no." Daddy took the letter and when he began to read it he started to cry. That was the first time I ever saw my Daddy cry. He just hugged Mama and they both just rocked. In a little while he composed himself and he told us the news. I must say my heart moved to my throat and I was all choked up. I couldn't believe it. No one said a word. In a little while Daddy looked at Mama and said, "Well, we've got to go up there."

The following Saturday morning Mama's back was feeling better, she packed a suitcase. She gave instructions to the younger children to mind our older sisters and brothers. They were in charge until Daddy got back. She had to go help take care of Mama Erna. Mama had tears in her eyes, I think because she had to leave us and the fact that her mother was so sick. She stayed a week and I know that was hard on her. The next Saturday Daddy went to get Mama and they returned home that Sunday. You could see the pain in Mama's eyes. When she sat on the sofa she looked so tired.

She called my two older sisters in the room where she was. They talked for a while and the decision was made that Willie Ruth would go help Aunt Luella with Mama Erna's care so Mama could continue to work. Willie Ruth stayed for about six months, with Mama relieving her in two-week sessions. Mama Erna was lasting longer that the doctors thought. They had given her only six months to live but it had already been six months. She was truly a fighter. It was the first of June 1965 and school was out. Mama asked me if I wanted to go to the Delta and help with Mama Erna. I was a little apprehensive at first and then I thought about how good my grandmother had been to me. Helping take care of her was just what I was supposed to do in good consciousness. I didn't know what I was going to be doing, but I was willing to learn.

I packed my bags and I was on my way to the Mississippi Delta. I was going back to Leland. I had not been to Leland in a while. Uncle Horse and Aunt Luella had gotten a divorce. They were the first black people I knew who had gotten a divorce, and to top that off my aunt had bought a house right next door to his house. That seemed like something right out of a television movie. Mama didn't quite understand that and said my aunt was acting as if she was a little touched in her head, meaning that her brain was not working quite right. My aunt Luella Davis was a world class cook in her own right and worked for the Dean family in Leland. When I got to Leland I could see that she lived very well. My grandmother was living with her.

Willie Ruth had sent a picture home of Mama Erna. She had lost quite a bit of weight. She was nearly bare skin and bones. I wasn't really shocked when I got there, but it did make me feel bad to actually see in person how frail she was. When I first got to my aunt's house I took a deep breath before I went into Mama Erna's bedroom. As I walked in her room I was smiling. Her eyes lit up like a candle and she smiled and said "There is Mama's Baby. "I just kept smiling with my heart breaking and I said "Yes, ma'am."

God Sent Us Angels In The Form of Good White Folks

Mama called me to the back porch and told me she would stay with me a few days to show me what had to be done. She told me to be very careful with everything and to make sure I washed my hands after everything I did. The first night I was there, my grandmother was having a lot of problems. Her stomach began to hurt and she was in a lot of pain. Mama showed me how to sterilize the needles to give my grandmother her morphine shots. I was terrified and with all of that she was unable to go to the bathroom. We had to make diapers to put on her out of sterilized white bed sheets, mama were nervous her hand was shaking. My aunt came in and gave my grandmother her shot and in about 30 minutes she was resting and finally went to sleep.

When Aunt Luella went to work, Mama and I cared for Mama Erna all the next day. She taught me how to give my grandmother a bed bath, help brush her teeth and comb her hair. Then she showed me how to sit her in a chair and change her bed and I mopped her room. Mama believed in concentrated Lysol and Clorox. As you remember, Mama was the Clorox queen. She stayed about three days and when she thought I knew everything I needed to know, Mama got ready to leave. Aunt Luella was there to show me the rest. I really hated to see mama go, but she had to go back to work.

The time I stayed with my grandmother was good for both of us. We got along really well and she was so glad I was there with her. I made her special foods for each of her meals and I served them on a tray just as I had for Mrs. Buford. I was used to making food trays look nice. On her tray I put some type of pretty flower to perk her up. She loved boiled okra and I fixed it just like she wanted it. Sometimes I put stewed tomatoes with it. Most of the time I baked her meats and of course lots and lots of sweet potatoes. It would get pretty lonely during the day sometimes. I read the Bible to my grandmother and she really liked that. I did the laundry every day. It seemed as if I was washing and washing all day but that's what it took to keep her clean. My aunt had a washing machine, so it was not so bad, and she had good steady clothes lines in the backyard.

Sometimes a few of her circle ladies from my grandmother's church would come and bring a casserole or other things to eat. That would give me a break from cooking. One day when one of the ladies was at the house she asked me if I would like for her to come and sit with Mama Erna so I could do something other than just be their all the time. Mama Erna told her that most of the children were in the cotton fields.

The lady said she thought I might want to go where the children were. Mama Erna looked at me and asked if I would like to go be with the children. I told her I would think about it. The lady told me my uncle had a truck and he took the children to the cotton field and I might get a chance to make a little money.

I don't think my grandmother liked that very much but I thought to myself that it wasn't a bad idea. I really liked to make my own money. The lady was still there when Aunt Luella came home from work so I asked my aunt if it was all right if I went to the field with Uncle Horse. She said that it was fine with her as long as somebody was with my grandmother. She said I could go one day a week. She called Uncle Horse for me and he said it was fine with him. She told me, "You know he comes about four o'clock in the morning?"

My grandmother told me how to dress for the cotton field. She said to put on a t-shirt, a long sleeved shirt, and long pants and to tie a rag around my head to keep the sweat from getting in my eyes. I also needed gloves and a wide brimmed straw hat. I thought that surely is a lot of gear. Aunt Luella gave me an alarm clock set for 3:30 a.m. and a long sleeved shirt, a straw hat and gloves. I already had my own blue jeans and a scarf. I was all set; I helped get my grandmother ready for bed. Then I went in the living room and let the sofa bed down. I was so excited that I was going to the cotton field to be with the children.

I was a little girl when we moved from the Delta and I didn't remember much about chopping or picking cotton. I only remembered the stories daddy use to tell us about me ridding his cotton sack, when I was a little girl. I did remember that it was what daddy called first light when they left the house to go to the field.

Chopping Cotton

It seemed as if Uncle Horse came as soon as I lay down. It was good that he came a little early. Aunt Luella got me up and I went in the bathroom, washed my face, and got dressed as fast as I could. I was ready in a flash. He had already picked up some people, adults as well as children. We sat on wood benches in the back of the truck that he had built and there was a top cover over the bed of the truck. I think everyone was too sleepy to speak but you know Mama had taught us to have good manners so when I got in I said "good morning to everyone." I barely heard the response but that was okay.

We drove for what seemed like hours to me. When we got a few miles outside of Leland down the highway, we turned off on a road where there was cotton on each side as far as I could see. I hadn't seen cotton like that since the sharecropping farm. We finally got to a turnoff and Uncle Horse had us to unload. He gave each one of us a hoe and assigned each of us a row of cotton. That row had to be five miles long. As we got started I noticed it was still dark and the sun was barely coming up. I hoped I wouldn't see any big bugs or snakes.

I didn't know what I was doing, so I just watched some of the others and caught on. I saw that they were chopping the grass from around the cotton. That was easy enough but some of the grass was pretty tall and after a while I got kind of confused and along with the grass I was chopping down cotton. The sun was up and I guess now Uncle Horse could see that I was chopping down the cotton. He ran down my row yelling for me to stop! He removed the hoe from my hand and told me to come with him to the truck. He gave me a water bucket and a ladle. He told me for the rest of the day I was going to be the water girl. I didn't mind because I was tired of chopping that cotton any way.

At straight up noon it was lunch time and Uncle Horse had us to load back up on the truck, he drove a few miles down the road. There was a general store on the side of the road. We all got out and went in to buy our lunch. The store reminded me of the store on Main Street in Leland. Aunt Luella had given me money to buy my lunch. For my seventy-five cents I got some lunch meat, crackers, cheese and a big giant Coke. It didn't take me long to get full. We were only there for a little while before it was time to go. I continued to be the water girl for the rest of the day. I must not have been thinking when I drank that big cola because it wasn't long before I had to go to the bathroom. As I looked around there was no bathroom to go to so I had to use the bathroom in the woods.

I was a wreck. There was this big oak tree in the far distance at the edge of the woods. It was wide enough to hide me. I saw other people leaving the woods so away I went. I got relief but you can bet I didn't drink anything else all day. When I got back some of the teenage children broke out singing church songs and "Go down Moses" was one of the songs. Everybody joined in and the songs kept coming, one after the other. That seemed to make the time go faster, it was fun. It was like something you see in old time movies.

We worked until almost sundown, when Uncle Horse called us all to the truck. I was mosquito bitten, suntanned, sweaty and exhausted. It was time for payday and I was so happy that the day had come to an end.

We waited patiently while uncle Horse was doing his tally to pay us. I was talking with one of the children who were with us. I wanted to know how much you were paid for working all day. She said we got three dollars a day, which was okay with me but that made me have a greater appreciation of working in Mama's Good White Folks Angels homes. Uncle Horse went around to every person and passed out the pay. After he finished we loaded on the truck and started home. Everyone was so tired we just all sat there and rode.

When I got home, I went straight to the bathroom and pulled off everything. I ran my bathwater and I sat in the tub, I know an hour. When I got out and got dressed, my grandmother asked me how my day was. I just looked at her and smiled. She asked me if I thought I'd go back again. I said I didn't think so. I talked to her for a long time. Her friend who had kept her stayed on a while. As we were talking she asked me what I wanted to be when I grew up. I said one thing I knew for sure. I knew I didn't want to be a cotton chopper. She and my grandmother both laughed. My grandmother said, "I want her to be a nurse because she really knows how to take care of me." She just didn't know how hard it was for me to see her that sick.

With each passing day my grandmother was getting frailer. Seeing her in that condition was taking a lot out of me. It was getting near the end of August, but my sixteenth birthday had been in July. Mama Erna had gotten her first Social Security check and she wanted to buy me something special for my birthday. I told her I didn't really want anything, I just really enjoyed taking care of her. She smiled and said "You are such a good girl God is always going to bless you." Aunt Luella took me shopping a few days later at the Sears and Roebuck store in Greenville a few miles from Leland. Aunt Luella told me that Mama Erna wanted to buy me something for school. I had told Mama Erna a few weeks before that I wanted a plaid kilt skirt with a big brass pin on the side, mama was going to get me for school. Aunt Luella let me buy two skirts and a beautiful white cotton blouse.

I used the money I made chopping cotton to buy some books, some 45 rpm records, and some headbands. When we got back home I showed Mama Erna what she had bought me. She was glad to have been able to do something for me. A few days after that Mama came. By that time Mama Erna was much weaker. Mama decided to let me go home because it was time to get ready for school. She told me she had a birthday surprise for me at home and that she was going to stay the rest of the time with her mother. The night before I left to go home Mama Erna had a really difficult time. Her pain level was breaking through the morphine. As I was lying in bed that night I heard her say "Come get me Jesus." I started to cry. I really hated to see her suffer so. As I laid there I began to pray and I asked God to "just don't let her suffer anymore, please just give her some rest."

The next day after eating dinner, that Sunday afternoon I got packed to leave. I had mixed emotions, a part of me wanted to stay and a part of me wanted to leave. It was hard but it was time for me to get ready for school. I said goodbye to Mama Erna and thanked her for everything and kissed her on her forehead.

As Daddy and I drove home, we didn't talk very much. I think he knew that Mama Erna wouldn't be with us much longer. When I got back home I was really tired, but I looked in the corner of the room where Mama told me to find my surprise. It looked like a gray box but as I investigated further I discovered it was a record player. I was so excited; I had my very own record player and could play my own records.

The remainder of the summer I was to work for Mrs. Buford while mama was with Mama Earn in Leland. I know it was hard on mama trying to help care for her mother, having to leave her children, husband and home. She was stronger than I ever imagine. I know mama was tired but she hung in there. When there is true love present it will give you strength to do the things that you have to do. Thank God for his ever loving presence through Jesus Christ and the Holy Ghost that gives us strength and courage to care for our love one and even strangers when necessary.

I know both how to be abased, and I know how to abound: everywhere and in all things I am instructed both to be full and to be hungry, both to abound and to suffer need. I can do all things through Christ which strengthened me. (Philippians 4:12-13) (New King James Version)

Sweet Sixteen

My sixteenth year birthday turned out to be a very sweet year. That's probably why they call it sweet sixteen. A few days after we were home, Daddy left to go back to the Delta. He and Mama stayed in Leland almost a month. That September Rosa had her baby and Mama Erna got an opportunity to see her first great grandchild, Vernon David Garner. Rosa said Mama Erna cried because she was too weak to hold the baby. A week later the phone rang and Daddy told us that Mama Erna had passed. When the phone call came, I was playing "Moon River" on my record player. As it was playing the tears were streaming down my face. I had the same knot in my throat and the same feeling in my stomach I had when President Kennedy and Medgar Evers were assassinated.

    I could take joy in knowing I had helped care for Mama Erna the whole summer and I had had a wonderful time with her. That gave me a sense of peace. My mother was a faithful daughter. She cared for her mother while making many sacrifices. The way she cared for her mother planted a deep seed in my spirit. After watching her, I prayed one day and asked God to let me be able to care for her and Daddy in their old age.

    After Mama Erna's funeral, things settled down a bit but Mama was going through a depression. However that wasn't the worst thing that was happening. Daddy learned that the man next door to us had bought the house that we lived in. We were going to have to move. Daddy looked for weeks and it took a while but he finally found a house. Daddy was always fortunate when the pressure was on. It never failed that God always made him a way out. Daddy truly trust in the Lord with his whole heart. I just don't understand how anyone could be so cruel knowing that my mother's mother had just died. Our neighbor had the nerve to go behind Daddy back and buy the house we were living in. Daddy and mama had always been so nice to all of our neighbors. Daddy just said "God must have a better place for us; God knows best in all things."

Our Move to Newport Street

The house was on Newport Street. It was 1965 and this time he was buying the house. What a blessing. Daddy said he just didn't want to be bothered like that again. Mama cheered up a good bit after that. She was going to have her very own house. I think we were all excited because we had never owned a house before. So I guess the wrong that was done to us had turned into something that was very good. It didn't take us long to get everything packed up. I did feel sad leaving the first friends I had made. I was going to miss the backyard parties, the wiener roasts and the neighbors in general.

I guess what I feared most was that I was going to have to start a new school and I wouldn't know anybody there. My brother William Joseph and I were the only children in the family in high school. Our new school was Brinkley Junior/Senior High on Livingston Road. Joe was in the 11th grade and I was starting 10th grade. Mama had the older children go over with her to clean the house before we moved in. We had to scrub that house from top to bottom.

We didn't mind. Everyone had a sense of pride. This was *our* house. We didn't have a lot of furniture so the move was easy. The house had two nice sized bedrooms, a nice sized living room and we had closets. This was much nicer than where we moved from. I was glad to see Mama so happy; she had a different attitude. I knew it must have made Mama and Daddy feel that now their work wasn't in vain. Although we did have to turn the dining room into a bedroom, Willie Ruth and I didn't mind. This was still better than Carnation Street. We had gone from three to four children per bed to just two per bed, and that was a wonderful thing. Willie Ruth and I were going to share a room. Since Rosa married, Willie Ruth and I did more things together socially. She was a junior at Jackson State and working at the University Hospital as a desk clerk and the King Edward Hotel where she was an elevator operator. The black workers had to enter through the back door. That was alright with her as long as she got her check to help pay for her tuition for school. My sister felt deep in her heart that she wouldn't have to enter through the back door the rest of her life.

Everything was working out. My baby brother was in elementary school and everybody was going to school. It was much easier for Mama to go to work now. She didn't have to worry about day care and paying out extra money. Mama still had time to get all of us off to school before she went to work. She also tried to make sure she got home before school was out.

Brinkley Junior/Senior High

My brother and I were in our new school and things were looking up. Brinkley was a very nice school building, much larger than Lanier. Mama went to school with us to register, because she wanted to keep up with our papers, birth certificates and shot records. When we got home, Mama told us that the principal of the school had been married to her cousin at one time. I didn't know whether that was a good thing or not. She assured my brother and me that Principal Sutton told her that he was going to keep a close eye on us. That didn't sound so good to me.

I had pretty nice teachers, but I didn't make many friends right off. I was still somewhat withdrawn. I tried to concentrate more on my studies. The school year passed without too many surprises and I did all right. I passed to the eleventh grade and that was all I cared about. When summer came Mama was still working for Mrs. Buford. She started working more for the Yelvertons while still putting some time in with Mrs. Cole and Mrs. Bailey.

Mr. Yelverton and Miss Ann had moved from their home on Naples Road off State Street and they needed a babysitter for the summer. Mama asked me if I wanted to work for them this summer. I said yes. They had a little boy Jimmy and a little girl Catherine and another child was on the way. That was my first long term babysitting job and I was sure I could do okay. I had helped with my baby brother. I had good babysitting skills. I had done some sitting for the Bailey's and they had two little babies their twin daughters. I was going to have work for the entire summer again

Mama told me to be sure to watch Jimmy and don't let him go to the lake in the Yelvertons Twin Lake Circle neighborhood. She said she never let him go to the lake when she was there because she was afraid he might fall in the water. I did as Mama said. I just kept Jimmy in the house and he didn't like that one bit. One day when I told him he couldn't go outside he looked me dead in the eye and said "I don't want you here. I want Rosie." I looked at him and told him, "I want Rosie too, but you still cannot go outside, if your parents are not home." Jimmy was a strong welled child. He folded his arms, pooch his mouth and stumped out of the room. He was the complete opposite of his sister Catherine.

Catherine was the sweetest quiet little girl. She was no trouble at all and she didn't talk very much. All she ever wanted me to do was help her bake a cake. I would get all of the ingredients together and put them on the counter where she could reach everything. She mixed her cake, put it in the oven and patiently waited for it to bake. Then she let it cool and put the icing on, pushed the finished cake back on the counter and just went back to her room.

I worked three days a week for the Yelvertons and whenever the Bailey's need me to babysit. It was really nice because everyone I worked for had air conditioning in their homes. It was nice and cool in their homes during the summer. We just had window fans at our house. At night Daddy would leave the front door open. The screen door would let the outside air in to help cool the house with the window fans blowing. It's funny how it didn't seem to be uncomfortable.

When you cleaned and ironed at work, you were cool. I did the cleaning and ironing when the children were napping. They were sweet children, easy to keep. I could get all my work done with a little time left over. Those were good summer jobs. Mama had favor with the people she worked for and her favor was turning out to be a blessing for me.

Mrs. Cole's Garden Party

One evening when I got home from work Mama said Mrs. Cole had called. She was having a garden party and needed someone to help serve. She asked Mama if I would help her. Of course I said yes, after all Mrs. Cole was still Santa Claus to me. She told Mama she was going to bring the uniform she wanted me to wear over to our house the day before the party.

The party was going to be the following Saturday Night. When Mrs. Cole came she brought a snow white uniform and a red and white checkered apron with a ruffle around it. The night I went to help Mrs. Cole, she had the most beautiful serving trays filled with fruit, congealed salads, berries and melons. She had made cantaloupe bowls, the cantaloupes were cut in half with vanilla ice cream inside for dessert. After the garden party was over Mrs. Cole came in the kitchen and told me that everyone thought I was adorable in my little maid's uniform. She was smiling from ear to ear. I was glad to be able to do something nice for her because she was so good to Mama.

The week after the party Mrs. Cole sent Mama home with a big bag of clothes. She had put a pretty cool-out outfit with a sailor collar on the top. Mama said Mrs. Cole said this is just for Clem. Most of the clothes Mrs. Cole gave Mama fit my younger sisters Dorothy and Cecilia. That was very sweet of Mrs. Cole to think of me, she had already paid me for helping her. That's just how Mrs. Cole was, but all of the people Mama worked for, were the same about giving her nice things.

I was blessed that Sissy and I were the same size and I could get all of her nice clothes. My younger sisters were blessed the same way with getting little Jane's clothes. We were very thankful that God had put so much compassion in the hearts of the white people mama worked for.

Mrs. Jane Cole
Winning at a Flower Show

Mrs. Cole on Vacation

Dear Rosie,

Mama's Church pictures just came and I thought you would like one.

Also, am enclosing a little check for you for Christmas. It'll be much different for all of us who loved her. This Holiday Season, I sure miss her and can't believe she's gone.

Thinking of you and wishing you happiness this Holiday and always

I know life goes on but it was surely much richer with her on earth.

Hope you're doing well + feeling ok

The Nutmeg Incident

One Saturday Mama went to work for Mrs. Buford to help her cook for her bridge club meeting. She and Mrs. Buford had made some orange cups from oranges cut in half and scooped out so they could be filled with mashed sweet potatoes. Mrs. Buford left the kitchen and played bridge for a while and returned to the kitchen and added nutmeg to the sweet potatoes. Mama said to her, "Don't you think you are putting too much nutmeg in there?" Mrs. Buford had drunk one too many highballs, she turned to Mama and said "You can never put too much nutmeg in." Mama replied "Yes ma'am".

When the meal was served, no one ate the sweet potato stuffed oranges. Mrs. Buford said to Mama, "Rosa, I wonder why no one at the orange sweet potato?" Mama told me she just kept working, and said in a low voice under her breath "Maybe it was the nutmeg." Mrs. Buford replied,"Oh, well."

Mama had many vivid accounts of the trials, tribulations and good times she and Mrs. Buford shared in their relationship. Mrs. Buford was strong-willed to say the least, but she knew Mama was faithful to her. Mama knew that she was the maid. She was also a strong woman and I am sure it was not a bed of roses all the times working in white homes, but she made it work for her. They both had a respect and understanding of their positions and relationship, which grew year after year into mutual love. As the years passed there was no separation, just a closer bond.

Mrs. Buford was getting packed for her cruise she was preparing to go on. Mama was helping her to get packed. Mama said Mrs. Buford looked at her and said "Rosa, why want you pack you bag or two and come and go on the cruise with me?" Mama turned and looked at Mrs. Buford with a smile and told her, "Yall got us over here on a boat one time, I am not getting on another boat, because ain't no telling where yall will take me this time." Mama said the both started laughing and they both were in tears they laughed so hard. I guess you know Mrs. Buford didn't invite my mama on anymore boat trips after that.

My Cup Was Full

Summer was over and school was about to start. We had one week left and I went to work with Mama to help because her back was still giving her trouble when she stood on her feet too long. While Mrs. Buford was getting ready for her trip, she had cleaned out closets. She told Mama she wouldn't have to stay too long. Mrs. Buford had put a stack of clothes and shoes from her and Sissy's closets on the sun porch for us to take home. She told Mama she wanted to thank me for helping with her grandchildren all summer.

When I started the eleventh grade it was hard to believe how fast time had passed. Truly good and great things had happened. Not only was I dressed to kill, as mama put it, I had some of the most wonderful teachers in every class. Of course the most difficult class I had was math. Mrs. Rogers was an older teacher, a stately lady. She had beautiful silk gray hair with a beautiful large braid that encircled her head much like a crown and gold wire rimmed glasses and she was very stern. She was no A. K. Lattimore but she was a good teacher. My speech teacher, Mrs. Joseph, was a jewel. My homeroom teacher Mrs. Adams was very good at getting us interested in English literature and Mrs. Celia Carr profoundly changed my life. She was the best music teacher in the world. I loved choral music, and she kept insisting that I could do better if I just tried harder in my class work, if I just applied myself. She let me know it was up to me.

In our speech class we all had to do an impromptu speech. Mrs. Joseph had been working with me on several of my speech projects. She was quite impressed after I had done one of my speeches. She called me over to her desk, and asked me if I would like to participate in an oratorical contest between the area high schools. She told me she thought I would do very well. She encouraged me to participate and told me she would give me extra credit. Extra credit sounded good to me, so I told her I would try. The next day Mrs. Joseph gave me the poem *"Lincoln, the Man of the People" by Edwin Markham.*

When I looked at that poem, I thought to myself, "You must be crazy." Mrs. Joseph must have seen the fear in my eyes, because she said, "Don't worry, I am going to help you with it, you are going to be fine." She told me the contest wasn't until late fall and we had plenty of time to practice, and practice we did. By the time it was time for the contest; I had memorized that poem and knew every line. Mrs. Joseph had helped me with all of the main expressions.

Time for the contest arrived, it was at my former high school, the very auditorium where I watched many other children perform. Never in my wildest dreams did I think I would be standing on that stage! There were only two people to speak before me. I can tell you one thing, I was as nervous as you get. But I kept my eyes focused on Mrs. Joseph and when they called my name and said "Now representing Brinkley Junior/Senior High…."

I stood proudly with the same grace that I had seen my older sister Rosa stand. I recited those three stanzas as if I had written them myself. When it was over, it was as if I had been in a dream state. I didn't win but I did take third place, in which Mrs. Joseph was very proud, and as a matter of fact I was too. Just think, the girl who almost fainted when asked to speak in front of a group of people, God gave her the courage to stand and not faint! I could also thank Mama because she never let us uses incorrect English at home or anywhere else. Mama knew people judged you by the way you dressed and spoke. Mama was wise, I tell you.

With that over, I was getting back to basics. I had joined the tennis team and was getting ready for our city championship. I had gained a wealth of confidence, and a little popularity with a few of my classmates; it was really a good feeling. I didn't realize that knowing people had confidence in you could make such a big difference in your life. People telling you that you could be whatever you want to be if you just tried. People actually showing you the path to accomplish what they're telling you means a lot in a child's life. I'm very thankful that I had people all around me showing me, like Mama and Daddy, my older sisters, and even the people mama worked for. Our school did well in the city tennis championship, though we didn't receive the title that year.

Things were really going well at school and at work. I was still working to earn my extra money, most of the time babysitting for Mr. Yelverton and Miss Ann, and I was working for the Bailey's when needed. On Saturday's I worked for Mrs. Buford. Mama worked so hard during the week that she was really tired on weekends. Most of the time I went to help at Mrs. Buford's on weekends. When I took her breakfast tray upstairs, if she was reading a book, she wanted to tell me about what she was reading. She said "Clementine" (she always called me by my full name). One morning she asked me to sit in a chair at the foot of her bed. She read to me from "1984" by George Orwell, she said the book was about a computer taking over the world and everybody's life. I just did know what a computer was.

It sounded science fiction to me. Mrs. Buford said "Can you imagine that?" I could not imagine that. She must have been really lonely because she read almost the whole book to me. Then she looked at me and said "Clementine, I want you to always read, that way you will know what is going on in the world." I said "Yes ma'am." Before then, I really didn't like reading, but after Mrs. Buford talked to me I started to read more, and she was right, I was learning more.

Teen Tempos

LINCOLN, THE MAN OF THE PEOPLE

by: Edwin Markham (1852-1940)

WHEN the Norn Mother saw the Whirlwind Hour
Greatening and darkening as it hurried on,
She left the Heaven of Heroes and came down
To make a man to meet the mortal need.
She took the tried clay of the common road--
Clay warm yet with the genial heat of earth,
Dashed through it all a strain of prophecy;
Tempered the heap with thrill of human tears;
Then mixed a laughter with the serious stuff.
Into the shape she breathed a flame to light
That tender, tragic, ever-changing face.
Here was a man to hold against the world,
A man to match the mountains and the sea.

The color of the ground was in him, the red earth;
The smack and tang of elemental things:
The rectitude and patience of the cliff;
The good-will of the rain that loves all leaves;
The friendly welcome of the wayside well;
The courage of the bird that dares the sea;
The gladness of the wind that shakes the corn;
The pity of the snow that hides all scars;
The secrecy of streams that make their way
Beneath the mountain to the rifted rock;
The tolerance and equity of light
That gives as freely to the shrinking flower
As to the great oak flaring to the wind--
To the grave's low hill as to the Matterhorn
That shoulders out the sky.

Sprung from the West,
The strength of virgin forests braced his mind,
The hush of spacious prairies stilled his soul.
Up from log cabin to the Capitol,
One fire was on his spirit, one resolve:--
To send the keen axe to the root of wrong,
Clearing a free way for the feet of God.
And evermore he burned to do his deed
With the fine stroke and gesture of a king:
He built the rail-pile as he built the State,
Pouring his splendid strength through every blow;

Sudie Gray's

The school year was ending and it was time for the seniors to have their class night program. Some junior class members served as hosts and hostesses for the class night program. After the program, some of the children wanted to go out for an outing. I was seventeen so Mama and Daddy said it was okay to go with my friends for a while, but I had a curfew of 11:30p.m. Several of us got together with our friend James Stokes, who had a car. There was a night club that teenagers went to occasionally called Sudie Gray's, which was off County line road after you passed Tougaloo College.

    I had never been to a club before. I was not familiar with drinking, but several of my friends were drinking what they called wine coolers. They asked me to taste one, and it tasted like Kool-Aid with ginger ale. I didn't think it was that bad. Our friends kept buying them and we kept drinking them. We were dancing and having such a good time, we didn't realize how quickly time was passing. But it was time for me to go, so everyone agreed and we left for home. To my surprise when I got in the bed, my head felt kind of woozy. That wasn't a good feeling at all. I had never felt like that before.

    Mama got up early the next morning and came to the door to tell me that Mrs. Buford needed me to help her that Saturday morning. Wow! I wasn't in the best shape but I had to go. When I got to work that morning, I was feeling really sick and my head was hurting so bad. I started as usual and got Mrs. Buford's breakfast tray ready and was headed upstairs. I got up to about the fourth step and slid back down those stairs. Poached eggs, orange juice, toast and all fell to the floor! Mrs. Buford yelled downstairs, "Clementine, are you all right?" I said "Yes ma'am, I just had a little accident, but everything is okay. I'll be up there in a minute." I guess you know I was beside myself. I got up as fast as I could, clean up the mess, and I do think I cooked the fastest breakfast in history.

By the time I got upstairs with Mrs. Buford's breakfast, she was sitting up on the pillows patiently waiting. I served her tray, and she said, "Sit here for a moment." I saw that she was reading another book. This time it was "Native Son" by Richard Wright. Surely, God was not going to let her read this book to me the way I was feeling. As she began to tell me about Bigger Thomas and what was going on with him, I thought I just might die right then and there.

She began to tell me the central point of the book. Just in the nick of time, the phone rang. She took the call and gestured that I could leave. I was one happy soul. Shortly after that phone call Mrs. Buford got dressed, put my pay on the counter and left. I finished cleaning the house, washed the dishes and called my ride. I was one sick girl.

When daddy picked me up he didn't say a word. He had this smirk of a smile on his face. When we got home, I walked in; daddy and mama were looking at each other. My mother said to me, "look like you don't feel good, is everything all right?" I just looked at her and said "yes, ma'am." She didn't fuss or anything. I guess she thought the way I was feeling was punishment enough. I got in bed and remained for the rest of the day, just sick! You can bet I did not want any more wine coolers again.

When I got back to school the next Monday, I told my friend Barbara I would never again touch another wine cooler. We both started to laugh, just as an announcement came over the intercom. The principal was announcing that Brinkley School had been chosen to be on Teen Tempos. That was a television program on WLBT Channel 3 where teenagers danced and performed talent acts. It was a Jackson, Mississippi version of American Bandstand.

A Star is Born

Brinkley was going to be the first black school to appear on the program. When I got to speech class, Mrs. Joseph came over to me and told me I had been chosen to do the same poem I did for the oratorical contest on TV. I thought to myself, "If I've done it once, I can do it again." When I got home that afternoon I told my parents I was going to be on television the following Saturday at five o'clock in the afternoon.

The next week when we got to school, everyone was so excited. The teachers had selected the students who were going to participate in the program. They took us down to the television station for a pre-taping. Everyone was very cordial to us. The taping went fine and that gave us an opportunity to see ourselves on T.V. the following Saturday.

I performed that poem with my whole heart. Mama had told Mrs. Cole, Mrs. Buford and everyone else about me being on television so they could watch. After the program aired that Saturday afternoon, our telephone started ringing. You would have thought I had been on Broadway. Everyone was so proud. Mama said Mrs. Cole told her, "Rosie Posy that Clem is something great." Mr. Gene told her, "Clem is so quiet I didn't know she had that in her."

Monday at school all the kids who had been on Teen Tempos automatically became the cool kids. There was something to be said about instant popularity. When it's positive, it can make a big difference in your life. Life is really strange. My sixth grade teacher attended church with Mrs. Joseph. Mrs. Joseph told me that she had told her, speaking about me, "I had no idea she had that in her." If she had just taken the time as Mrs. Joseph did, she would have known what was in me. The school year ended on a very positive note. God had blessed me to find something within myself, through others who had confidence in me. I passed to the twelfth grade and I was very thankful.

Change in Mississippi

This was going to be the 1966-67 school year and all of the schools in Mississippi were still segregated. There has been a great migration of white students into private schools. Our officials paid no attention to the federal desegregation laws. We have always had cultural differences which, for the most part, seemed normal to us. I never believed that I was less of a person because I didn't attend school with white children. As a matter of fact, I never thought about it.

God has always put a spirit in us as a people to use what we have to the best of our ability and He will do the rest. We had used text books, but they had the same information in them. We had to take nothing and make something out of it. That is called survival and as the old adage goes, only the strong survive.

Things were changing slowly, but they were changing. Some people, like our counterparts in other areas of Mississippi were having it much worse than the black folks in Jackson. Many of them did not attend school at all, and lived as if they were in third world countries. They were stuck in low paying jobs or no jobs at all, but then some blacks in north Mississippi were doing well. My mother's uncle Percy Pattison was one of the largest black farmers in the Mississippi Delta. Dr. Helen Barnes a black gynecologist had opened a clinic in North Mississippi to promote better health for black women.

There were cotton fields in rural areas outside of Jackson, but we had a choice of working in the cool air of a white person's home, teaching school, being a nurse, or being a school administrator, lawyer, doctor, business owner or going to the field. Our schools had heat and some had air. We could shop on Farish Street where most of the black businesses were. We also had the Alamo Movie Theater. While we were fighting for equal rights, we were counting our blessings and God was keeping us. The important thing is that we had work and we had God. Many negative opinions came from ignorance of not searching for the truth. All black and white relationships were not completely negative.

I was a maid and a babysitter of white children. I learned so much while working in those homes and so did my mother. My mother patterned her life from some the white women she worked for. She was intelligent, caring, funny and a lady. She took the best behaviors from those women and integrated them into her own personality. I think she did very well. I really liked my job babysitting. I had to do housekeeping and some ironing, but mostly just tending the children, which I believe was pretty easy. I also think it made me a better mother to my own children. I went to Mrs. Cole's sometimes to help her iron. The experience made me able to iron better than most dry cleaners. My mother enjoyed having a way to help provide for her children.

Mama knew that working for Mrs. Buford was going to soon change when school was out and Sissy left. Mrs. Buford wouldn't need her as much. Mr. Gene asked Mama to come to work for them and help with the children. He really liked having Mama around for that good home cooking and he knew that she was really good with the children. Mr. Yelverton had adopted Mama as his other mother. He would often tell her, "Rosie, you are part of this family." They both loved to cook and they had as much fun in the kitchen cooking as Mama and Mrs. Bailey did. It is strange to me how a little thing like cooking together can build such a strong bond between people. I guess it is true that the kitchen is the heartbeat of the home.

God Sent Us Angels In The Form of Good White Folks

The last Sunday dinner Mr. Yelverton had at his home on Naples Road, I went to work with Mama to help. She and Mr. Gene made a roasted pork loin, sweet potato casserole, corn pudding, greens, cornbread sticks and rum-raisin bread pudding for dessert. That was a masterpiece of a meal. It was like watching artists at work. Every seasoning had to be just right. I tell you, it was something to see two masters at work. Mr. Yelverton and Miss Ann were celebrating moving into their new house on Twin Lakes Circle. Mama said they needed more help because they were getting ready to have another child and there was going to be lots to do with a new baby and a big new home. When the family had finished eating, I helped mama clear the dinner dishes from the table. As I rinsed the dishes mama loaded them in the dish washer and when she got the dish washer full. We began to wash the pots and pans; with us working together we were finished in a flash.

We finished just in time, I looked out the window of the back door and daddy was driving up. Mama knew she had to hurry because daddy didn't like to wait and sometimes his short temple would make him start to blow his horn. Mama hated when he did that, she would be so embarrassed. In about 10 minutes or so we finished up with pots and pans and put everything away. To our surprise daddy didn't start to blow his horn. Mama said "uh, I wonder what wrong with him?" Ms Ann came in the kitchen with mama's pay, she was giving mama her pay as she looked out the window and saw daddy outside. She told mama "Rosie, Bill is out there and he is not blowing, mama said "yes ma'am that is something" and they both laughed, that was some kind of inside joke.

Daddy was sitting there just as patient; he even had a smile on his face. His calm spirit was quite a bit out of the norm, because most Sundays he would have been watching a ballgame or listening to one on the radio, it upset him to break from his game time to come pick mama up from work. It was nice to see him in such a good mood and I know mama was as happy as could be.

Mama told him "you sure look nice today where have you been?" He chuckled a little and said "you would never guess." He told mama, he had met Rev. PD Howard and he invited him to visit his church. Howard's Chapel on Idaho Street was not far from where we live. Daddy told her that was not the first time he had been to church at Howard's Chapel. Daddy could see by the expression on mama's face that she was not quite happy with what he had said. Daddy's quick wit immediately made him say but I'm not going back until you can go with me.

Daddy Found Jesus

Mama asked how church was and he said he had really enjoyed it. Mama just said "That's good," and that was the end of the conversation. When we got home, Mama and I went into the house. Daddy stayed on the porch reading his Bible. Mr. Yelverton had given us dinner to bring home, so Mama didn't have to cook. Mama prepared Daddy's plate, put it on the table and called him in to eat. As we sat at the table while Daddy was eating, he had a different look about himself.

The next day when Daddy got home from work, he was sitting on the front porch reading the Bible. I came out of the house to see what he was doing and he looked at me and said, "Clem, bring me the garbage can." To my surprise Daddy, who chewed Brown Mule Chewing Tobacco, smoked George Washington Cherry Blend Pipe Tobacco, and drank, stopped all his vices cold turkey. I can tell you that was something to see. But the granddaddy of them all was when he announced to Mama he had been called to preach. Daddy told Mama that God had been blessing him so abundantly; he wanted to spend the rest of his life working for the Lord. Mama was so happy. That is one time my Mama was at a total loss for words.

Our life on Newport Street was bringing about a lot of changes. Daddy found Jesus and mama was starting a job with another generation of Mrs. Buford's family. I found a talent I didn't know I had the courage to speak in front of large groups of people. The little girl who was so nervous when she spoke in public, who had panic attacks that almost made her pass out, was now able to speak in front of hundreds of people with little or no fear. **That had to be God!**

While mama was working full time for Mr. Yelverton and part time for the Bailey's, I was going to help Mrs. Buford on Saturdays only. Sissy was getting ready to go to flight attendant's school for American Airlines. I thought that was so glamorous. I was happy for her, but I sure was sad to see her go. It really was going to be lonely in that big house without her.

When I got to work that morning, her bags were all packed, but she wasn't home. I served Mrs. Buford her breakfast, and she had yet another book to share with me. This time it was "Animal Farm" by George Orwell, and now the animals were taking over the world. I guess you know I had to sit again and listen as she explained the theme of the book to me. After she had finished, she asked me what I was planning to do when I got out of school. I told her I wasn't sure.

She explained to me how important a good education was. She made a lot of good points and the seed was planted. Daddy and Mama had told me the exact same thing. I knew I needed a good education, I just didn't know how to go about getting it; I was doing all I knew to do. I was doing much better, simply because I was trying harder.

I guess with Sissy leaving, Mrs. Buford didn't want to be home to experience her empty nest syndrome, so she planned herself another trip. This time she was getting ready to go out to California to visit her daughter and her family. She said that she was going to make sure the house was cleaned and in order before she left, because she was going to be gone for at least a month.

Surprise....Surprise....Surprise

A week or so later, I went to do a little cleaning for Mrs. Buford. When I went to clean Sissy's room, it was in shambles. I dusted the furniture, hung clothes in the closet and started to vacuum, as I was vacuuming under her bed, I hit something. I got down on my hands and knees and looked under the bed. I just couldn't believe my eyes. I was just stunned!!!! Sissy had been a bad girl. I didn't tell Mrs. Buford, Mama, or anybody else. To this very day I have never told a soul. And I never will unless Sissy gives her permission.

I had worked most of the summer and didn't have a lot of leisure, but all in all it was a good summer. It was coming to an end and I had done well working. Mama was really happy. She had helped Mr. Yelverton and Mrs. Ann get moved. They had purchased new furniture, so they gave mama some their old furniture but it was like new. One chair in particular that they had bought in England and a set of dining room chairs. Mama was so proud of those chairs that she wouldn't let us sit in them. She had the seats covered in plastic so they would not get soiled.

Just before school started, Mrs. Buford called mama to come help her serve her bridge club brunch. Mama worked only a few hours that Saturday and Mrs. Buford sent all the clothes Sissy had left at home to me. I didn't have to buy a thing. Mama couldn't thank Mrs.

Buford enough. Daddy was right, God was blessing us more than we could ever imagine.

At the beginning of the 1967 school year we moved to new Brinkley High School on Albemarle Road we still had to walk to school. We had most of the same teachers from our old school, which was good. With all of them familiar with the students, we should have a pretty easy year. My brother had graduated in the class of '66. I was the only family member in high school that year. My two younger sisters Dorothy and Cecilia were attending Powell Junior High in our old school building on Livingston Road.

I loved all of my teachers, except my history teacher. I was taking all the classes I needed for college prep. My English Literature teacher passed out the list of books we needed to read for the year and to my surprise the list contained "Native Son", "1984", "Animal Farm", "To Kill A Mockingbird", and some poems from Greek mythology. (**Kudos**) to Mrs. Buford. Thanks to the wise woman who critiqued every book she got her hands on and thought enough of me to share them. I had a heads up on all of the books I needed to read for the school year.

The school year passed quickly, I guess it is true the more fun you have, the faster time flies. For the first time, I really enjoyed my classes and school. We were invited to be on Teen Tempos again and this time I was chosen to do the Teen Report, talking about the things that were going on in our high school. We were a big success again and everyone congratulated us. Mama got calls from everybody she knew telling her how much they enjoyed the show and seeing me on TV again.

Daddy was working year round now. He had built a steady list of clients for his yard-cutting business and was driving a school bus during the school term. Mama was working for Mr. Yelverton and Miss Ann, who by then had four children. Besides Jimmy and Catherine, there was Little Gene and Edward. The Bailey's had four girls. Mama was there caring for her Good White Folks Angels babies, as she put it.

God Sent Us Angels In The Form of Good White Folks

The last time I babysat for the Yelvertons was at his parents' house the Easter before school was out my senior year. I don't remember counting the number of children that were there, but it was close to twenty I know. They had a very large backyard. We must have hidden five hundred Easter eggs and the children had a ball looking for them. That was truly the largest family gathering I had ever attended.

There were many first for Mama, daddy and our family as a whole on Newport Street and there were many first for Brinkley High School and for me. Brinkley was the first black school to appear on Teen Tempos. Our senior class of 1967 was the first graduating class from the new Brinkley High School. We were the first black school to graduate in the Coliseum and I was the first black student to give the graduating speech in the Coliseum. As I look back, our family had come a mighty long way, through mistreatment, hardships and pain. I was praying for a miracle, to get into college, because I really wanted to go.

When mama came home from work at the Yelvertons she told me she had a surprise for me. She said she was talking to Mr. Yelverton about how hard it was going to be for Daddy and her to send me to college. Mr. Yelverton told her not to worry, that everything was going to be all right. He had been thinking of something nice to get me for a graduation gift, and he and Ms Ann thought they would love to help you go to college.

Mama was full of joy; she kept saying "Thank You Lord." She looked at me and said, "You see when you work hard, show respect and have good manners how people want to do nice things for you." "Always remember that." "Your attitude can make or break you." As mama was talking, I was thinking to myself how glad I was that I had listened to her and taken her good advice, and how wonderful it was that God had answered my prayer for a miracle.

Jackson, Mississippi, 1967

When the time came for me to leave for college, Rosa and Willie Ruth were just as excited as I was. Rosa and Lee bought me a psychedelic pink set of luggage which had different designs and colors on it. Willie Ruth bought my trunk. Mrs. Buford had Mama bring me over to her house, and when I got there she had gotten me clothes, some of them brand new. She even made her best friend, Mrs. Clementine Brown, bring me some clothes. Daddy's truck was loaded and we still had to go by Mrs. Cole's house. She had gotten me sheets, pillowcases and a bed spread.

The Sunday morning when I got ready to leave for school, Mr. Yelverton and his father drove up in his big black car. I was surprised to see them. Daddy loaded my bags in the trunk. Mr. Gene looked at Mama, who had tears in her eyes, and said, "Don't worry Rosie; she is going to be just fine." I gave Mama a hug and a kiss and got in the back seat of the car and away we went, up Highway 49 North, to Itta Bena, Mississippi, to Mississippi Valley State College.

The drive was very pleasant. Mr. Gene started making small talk. He was telling me about how beautiful some of the buildings were on Valley State Campus. I guess he could tell I was nervous. When we got to the campus, he drove around and showed me all the nice buildings, some of which he had designed. That's when he told me he was an architect. Then we drove to a large brick house.

God Sent Us Angels In The Form of Good White Folks

Mr. Yelverton told me he wanted me to meet the President of the college, Dr. White. We went in and he introduced me to President White and his wife. They were not surprised to see me. It was as if they had been waiting for us. The one thing that was amazing to me was that Mrs. White's hair was blue. They were very nice people. I did notice that they were both very fair skin people, almost white.

They chatted for a while, and we left and went to the freshman women's dormitory. Mr. Gene and his father brought my bags into the dorm. He told me I was already registered. Then he went into his wallet and gave me some money. He told me if I needed the least thing to just give him a call. He said, "All I want you to do is to study hard and make good grades." I thanked him and his father and I gave Mr. Gene a hug and they left. Never in my wildest imagination would I have thought that someone would do something so very special for me.

All of that semester I worked very hard my roommate Shirley and I spent a lot of time in the library. We pulled all nighters and weekenders until we knew all the subject matter in every subject. My track record for not liking to study changed with the right motivation. That first semester I was on the President's List. I called my mother to tell her about my good grades. I explained to mama that I had made all "As." She was so proud of me that she started to cry. I told her I hoped those were tears of joy and she said they were. "God bless Mr. Gene, I just thank God for him." She told me to be sure to call him and tell him the good news. She knew he would be just as proud of me as she was.

I called Mr. Gene to tell him about my grades and my making the President's List. He sounded so happy for me. In a soft voice he said, "Clementine, I knew you could do it. Keep up the good work and let me know how everything goes." Then he asked me if I needed anything. I told him "no sir," and thanked him for everything again. Then I said goodbye.

The new semester started, and before we knew it, it was time for the holiday break. As we prepared to go home, everyone was in high spirits. The day Daddy and Mama came to Valley State to pick me up was the first time the dormitory matron had seen my parents. Mrs. Johnson was quite inquisitive and wanted to know what type of work my parents did. I couldn't see what that had to do with anything, so I just told her I couldn't really say. That increased her level of curiosity, even more I know.

I was excited because I had never been away from home on my own before and I had become extremely homesick. Mama was all smiles, and I could tell that Daddy was proud. I introduced them to my roommates Shirley and Joyce. They asked me how I had been, because when I wrote them, I didn't say much in my letters except that the food was not the best. It was nothing like I was used to eating at home because Mama's cooking was the best. We talked for a little while and then Shirley's mother came in. She was a school teacher at Summer Hill School in the Clinton school system back home. Soon we said our goodbyes and left for home.

When we got home, I was a little tired. My younger sisters and brothers were glad to see me and I got lots of hugs. My oldest bother smiled and asked me when was I going to cook him some of my famous fried chicken. I laughed and told him my chicken cooking days were over. He said, "Yeah right." I must say I had become a pretty good cook. I guess the talent was passed down to me. All that time watching Mama and her "Good White Folks Angels" cooking had rubbed off on me. Mama had the nicest dinner that day. I surely had missed her rutabagas, corn bread, and baked sweet potatoes with neck bones on the side. Now that is some good eating.

Many times we don't appreciate the simple things in life until we don't have them anymore. When I was away from home, I often thought about those wonderful hot meals. No matter how meager they were, in my mind they seem like exotic cuisine. We should not miss any opportunity to be thankful for just the simple things. I had for many years tasted some of the best food that was ever prepared, thanks to mama's "Good White Folks Angels." But still, some of my mother's simple meals were just as good, because they were so satisfying.

I Saw Hate

The holidays were just what I needed to rest up. I had no idea how tired I was. Those all night study sessions Shirley and I had pulled had taken a toll on me. I didn't open a book the whole time I was home. We had a nice Christmas and New Year's. Mama had worked for Mr. Gene and Miss Ann during the holidays and they had sent me an envelope with some money in it for my spending money at school. My mother's "Good White Folks Angels" just kept on blessing me.

The Sunday after New Year's, it was time to go back to school. My neighbor Fannie Spann and I rode back to school together. Her brother drove us. We got hungry and saw a Frost Top Fast Food Restaurant off the highway, if memory serves me well. We drove through the drive-through window. A white woman came to the window and said, "We don't serve Niggers." James said to her, "We don't eat them." She replied, "You Niggers better get away from this window before I call the High Sheriff on y'all." We left, but I never forgot that experience. That was my first real encounter with one-on-one verbal racism. Of course we drove off, but none of us were hungry any more. That was enough to take your appetite.

For a few minutes there was silence. We were shocked and didn't know why. All of us knew racism existed, but I guess being confronted with it so unexpectedly caught us off guard. I thought to myself, "What is it that could make a human being hate another human being so much, when they didn't even know each other?" It just didn't make sense to me. In a way I felt sorry for that woman. I hated *what* she did, but I just couldn't hate *her*. Was something wrong with me? The thing was, I had been around white people all my life, and none of them had ever said anything ugly to me or treated me badly.

When we got back on campus, I went to my room, but no one was back. I was still thinking about what had happened. I prayed, "Please Lord don't ever let my heart hate like that. I don't want to be in that condition." Shortly after I had prayed, Shirley came in the room. She must have sensed something was wrong. She asked how my holiday had been and I told her it was great. "Well, what's wrong?" she asked. I told her what had happened and she said, "That's something you can't do anything about. It's been that way since the beginning of time, people hating people because of race, religion, color or just for no reason at all. You just have to learn to live with it." Then she smiled and said, "Let it go, pray for the lady and let it go." So I prayed for the lady again. I just asked the Lord to help her, and I let it go. January was so cold. It snowed with sleet and ice mixed. I guess God was trying to freeze the hate and hell out of the hearts of some of us down here on earth.

The winter was so cold. It seemed as if spring would never come. Classes were going very well. Shirley and I hit those books really hard. We had what was called a tele-lecture class, televised from Mississippi State University. We had to do a once a month campus visitation to Mississippi State University's campus at Starksville. We dreaded it because the white students looked at us as if we were from another planet. The class was our biology course and we needed those credits badly, so we had to go. I was glad when mid-term came and it was over.

My speech professor Dr. Musgrove had cast me in the campus production of "Our Town." I had the leading lady role of Emily. The leading man who played my husband was from Trinidad, his name was Michael. His friend Wilham Joseph was in the play also.

God Sent Us Angels In The Form of Good White Folks

I loved their accent. Shirley told me in the scene when I died from child birth and came back as a spirit, and my mother couldn't see me as I was pleading with her to look at me, that she started to cry. I must have been a good actress, if I made Shirley cry. After the production, it was back to hitting the books. We were heading for the last roundup. It snowed that March and it was not fun walking to class in the bitter cold.

April started out really chilly, but things seemed to be going as smooth as ever. On April 4 1968 Shirley and I had just come from the student union when we heard all this loud noise coming from outside our dorm. We looked out of the window and all of the students were screaming and crying. Joyce came in our room and told us Dr. Martin Luther King had been killed in Memphis. Everybody was in an uproar. Mrs. Johnson wasn't at the desk in the lobby, so we all left the dorm and went outside with the other students. The upper class boys built a huge bonfire and started singing freedom songs. We stayed out a long time and we all missed curfew. Mrs. Johnson locked us out of the dorm. When we finally decided to go back to the dorm, we couldn't get in. Mrs. Johnson came over and unlocked the door. As we entered, she had a sign-in sheet for us to sign.

The next day, as we were getting ready to leave the dorm, she stopped us to tell us that everybody who was on the sign-in list from the previous night was placed on social probation. She said we had all broken the school regulation of curfew. No one on the list could receive visitors, meaning boyfriends not coming over to our dorm. Shirley and I really didn't care because we weren't dating anyway. We had just gotten caught up in the emotion of it all. We were using that time to let out pain and anger. We were hurt and mad. As my roommates and I discussed what had happened, we all started to cry. We just wanted all the killing to stop and we didn't know what we should do.

Then Shirley said something that brought us back to reality. She said that Dr. Martin Luther King would have wanted us to act with the best behavior ever. He would want us to be peaceful, to act and do what he stood for - non-violence. Shirley made a lot of sense. After she got through talking, she said, "Let's all pray." We prayed for Dr. King's family, for peace, unity, our state and our nation. A young lady that lived in our dormitory that was from Athens Georgia named Olivia, who favored Aretha Franklin and sung like her too started to sing the Negro Anthem, and by the end of the song many of the children were crying. That was one emotional moment I can tell you.

Just when I thought things couldn't get any worse, Mama sent me a letter telling me that my oldest brother had been in a bad car wreck. He had broken nearly every bone in his body, and was in a body cast. She said they had waited to tell me, because at first the doctors told them he was not going to make it. She didn't say it, but I knew I had to go home when school was out. Shirley and I had planned to go to summer school to speed up our finishing college. This circumstance had altered our plans completely.

Time had passed and spring semester was at an end. I had the most fascinating year in my life. My grades were better than I could ever imagine. The experiences I had, helped me to mature and know I could live away from home and survive. I had so many people to thank for helping me get to that point in my life. I thanked God first and foremost for helping me make good choices, and not letting me die from the food in the cafeteria and adjusting to those grab bags they gave us for our evening meal on Sundays. I also thanked Mama and Daddy and all of Mama's "Good White Folks Angels, especially Mr. Gene Yelverton. They helped me understand that all white people are not evil folk tale devils who hate all black people.

My Return Home

When I got home, my brother was just as Mama had said. He was in a hospital bed and had casts on both legs, all the way up to his chest and arms. Mama had him so clean, he was shining. His bed sheets were as white as snow. I hated to see him in that condition. I could tell mama was so happy to see me and I knew she was glad to have some more help. My two younger sisters were no longer home. Cecilia and Dorothy had graduated high school. Dorothy had gone to California to school and Cecilia had gotten a scholarship to Tougaloo Collage and was living on campus. Willie Ruth was away at the University of Florida getting her Masters.

The only children home now was Anthony, my baby brother Lynn and my oldest brother. The first thing my oldest brother asked me about was fried chicken. I told him if he was still thinking about food, that nothing was wrong with him and we both laughed. I was happy to be home. I must say I had missed the gang. I helped Mama during that night with my brother. He had to use a bed pan, and with all that armor on, he was heavy. He had a lift over the bed and he tried to help us as much as he could. There was not must he could do because he had cast on both arms.

When I was all settled in and got rested a little mama was able to get back to work. She had been going to work when someone could be home with William Alfred. It was no easy job caring for him, but we had to do what we had to do. I saw how hard caring for my brother and working had been on Mama. I knew her back was stressed to no end. But she just did what she had to do with caring for one of her children. Daddy was strong; he could pick up my brother up as if he was a newborn baby. He would put him in a wheel chair to carry him to his checkup at the hospital. The doctors at the University of Mississippi Medical Center were doing a wonderful job and caring for my brother. This was 1968 and I don't think my brother could have gotten better care anywhere else than he was getting right here in Jackson.

Willie Ruth had worked at the University Hospital as a desk clerk, and babysat for some of the black school teachers here in town before she graduated from Jackson State and took her teaching job in Amory up in north Mississippi. I needed to work because I was going to start school at Jackson State College in the fall. Mama had Mr. Yelverton, Mrs. Buford and Mrs. Cole covered. Mrs. Buford no longer had children at home, nor did Mrs. Cole. Mama was trying to make up the time she had missed at work caring for my brother. She worked as much as possible to help daddy with the bills. I would work for the Yelvertons when Mama had to go to the doctor with my brother, and some weekends. That was not enough days to work, so I asked my sister to refer me to some of the teachers she had worked for.

Willie Ruth had referred me to Dr. and Mrs. Greenfield to baby-sit. Dr. Greenfield was the Dean of Instruction at Jackson State College. Mrs. Greenfield was in school working on her Master's degree. She had been in the military and was going to school on her G. I. bill. She had told me this while she was interviewing me for the baby setting job. She told me about all the places she had gone during her tours of duty. The Greenfield's had two small daughters. They had transferred to Mississippi from Greensboro, North Carolina's A & T. University. They lived in a new subdivision off Livingston Road on Rockdale Street, where a lot of prominent blacks lived at

God Sent Us Angels In The Form of Good White Folks

that time. Their home was a beautiful two story house. All of the appliances were pink, and I mean everything, from the washer and dryer to the stove and refrigerator – all of them, it blew my mind. Mrs. Buford was right: if you get a good education and work hard, you can own buildings and have a nice home. I saw that for myself. It was a good job. Mrs. Greenfield was down to earth, very easy to talk to. I learned a lot while working for the Greenfields.

When Mrs. Greenfield left in the mornings, her beautiful home became mine in my imagination. I got busy cleaning, cooking and just enjoying myself. Most of the time when the girls got up, about 9:30 a.m, I was through cleaning, and I had lunch on. I was the perfect housekeeper and baby sitter. I fed the children their breakfast, gave them their bath, and then I would take them out side to get some fresh air and play a while just as I did with the Yelvertons' children. My baby sitting skills were really paying off. It is really amazing how your environment can change your whole attitude. I worked for the Greenfield's and their next door neighbors, Dr. George Washington and his wife Dora, another black family. They also had two children, a boy and a girl, who I would baby-sit from time to time. Both of those black families lived very well. That gave me a sense of knowing exactly what I had to do to live as well as they did. The key was education and hard work. (**But always God first**)

I rode the city bus to school every day. In those days we didn't worry about getting a car because that was just not in the plan for most black children. My bus stop was on the corner of Lynch and Rose Streets. There was a little soul food restaurant called the Penguin at the corner Dalton and Lynch where you could get a breakfast of grits, toast, scramble eggs and a cup of coffee for a dollar. That was one good hot breakfast in the morning. The Penguin was a blessing to many students. That dollar breakfast kept many students going all day long. They also had a lunch special which consisted of a hot dog, French fries and a drink, for one dollar.

When I started at Jackson State, I was on work study, and with my other financial aid, I was able to manage my college expenses.

Dr. Greenfield gave me a job in his office as an office assistant, I had everything I needed. I was working two other part time jobs while going to school. This was taking a toll on me. I was taking more courses and my studies suffered. After all, I didn't have a friend like my roommate Shirley to keep me grounded. I was falling behind in my coursework and it was a disaster.

Dr. Greenfield was checking on me closely. When he found out that my grades were falling, he told me that I had to make some decisions, and I had to pull my grades up. If not I would not be able receive work study or continue school. It was awful. I had to make a conscious decision to change my lifestyle and commit to studying harder to pull myself out of this horrible rut. It was going to take me making all "A's" or nearly all "A's" to pull my average up to at least a "C."

I started to pray, and I asked God to help me, I was crying and shaking my stomach was in knots. I was so afraid I was not going to be able continue school. I thought back to all the good study habits I had developed with Shirley. Surely God would not let me come this far and fail. Surely He would help me find a study partner, or maybe He just wanted me to do this by myself, to let me know that He was in charge. I kept my work study job and my baby setting. The jobs that I had working at Summers Subway Lounge and the Alamo movie theater I quit. I was working too long at night and didn't have time to study. Mama had already told me that, but sometimes as a young person you can get hooked on the money aspect, and it's hard for you to accept wise council. I didn't want my parents to find out, because they would be so disappointed in me.

I was fortunate that year because I was taking most of my psychology courses. Special Education was my major with a minor in Psychology. I loved psychology. I was learning so much about how the human mind worked. The mental, emotional, and biological function of the brain was fascinating to me.

God again had placed a very special professor in my path. Doctor Charles Mosley, who was my statistics, testing measurements, and evaluation professor. He had gone over some of my papers, and asked me to remain after class because he needed to discuss one of my papers with me. He told me that in his years of working with many students, and from some of his major new studies on learning disabilities, it seemed to him that the problem I was having with my coursework, and especially formulating ideas and writing, seemed to show that I may have a condition that was call dyslexia. He explained to me that dyslexia was a type of learning disability.

That simply meant that the way I look at signs and symbols somehow got scrambled in my brain, and I had to find a way to decode the types of signs and symbols that I was trying to recognize. I asked him if the disorder was a mental illness and he said "no by no means. You just have to find a method that works for you that will make you understand those signs and symbols better, and retrieve them when needed. It might just mean that you have to study harder and longer." That is just what I did, study harder and longer. I felt as if Dr. Mosely had saved my life. Of course you know my mind was doing roller coasters, but I settle down and just thanked God for another opportunity to get back on track. And again God has sent a very special teacher who took the time to find out why I was having difficulty.

God prepared my heart and mind to go into hard core study. I didn't let up. I studied day and night and God brought me through. I did in fact make nearly all "As." I had taken 20 hours and had made a "B." in only one course. My average came up and I was off of academic probation. I know, and I hope you know, that for me was a miracle. From that time on, I was able to make good decisions that benefited my education.

Things were going very well at school by the spring of 1970. That was my senior year and I was as happy as I had ever been while attending school. I was doing more babysitting, which gave more time to study. Not only did I have the black families that I worked for, but was back helping the Yelvertons! Mama worked primarily during the week and I would help out on weekends.

Mama was really happy that I had stop working nights because she thought it was unsafe. I must admit that it was much easier on me to just do my babysitting to earn money as well as my work study, on campus job. That was quite enough. I was still working extremely hard on my studies and did fine by myself, doing a lot of late night study.

Our Psychology Department Heads had selected a group of students that they were going to take to a Psychology Conference in Chicago. I was one of the students that were selected. The conference was going to be held during spring break to insure that we wouldn't miss any classes. It would be my first time going to Chicago, and it was also my very first time attending a professional conference. The best part was the school was paying for everything for the trip. We were only responsible for our meals. I had heard mama and daddy on countless occasions speak of the relatives that we had in Chicago, but I had never met any of them. Daddy had a sister that lived there with her daughter. My mother's aunt Martha and her daughter also lived in Chicago. Daddy and mama both had many colorful stories about the relatives that lived up north. I truly had hopes in my spirit that I would get an opportunity to meet some of them. Daddy never had enough money to take a long vacation, and as it was, none of the relatives came down to Mississippi to visit us much either.

The way to keep in touch with family members doing that time was to write letters frequently, to let family members know how they were doing. However, my grandmother Mama Erna would go to visit all of the relatives up north from time to time. She would let the rest of the family know how everybody was doing.

We were going by train to Chicago on the Illinois Central. I was very excited about the train ride. Mama had mentioned a time or two that we had ridden a train before. We would ride from Hattiesburg to Leland to visit my grandmother, but I was much too young to remember, so you can imagine my excitement, a young woman leaving Mississippi going up north for the first time. I was still being

God Sent Us Angels In The Form of Good White Folks

blessed by Mr. Yelvertons' gifts, and was still thanking God for him, Mrs. Buford and Mrs. Cole.

It was the first of March, time for spring break and time for our trip to Chicago. There were 10 students that were going on the trip to the conference, as well as five of our psychology professors. We're going to stay at the Conrad Hilton Hotel. That was also my first time staying in a hotel.

Mama was as excited as I was. She had given me the phone numbers of some of our relatives and Carolyn Bass. My mother wanted me to check on them, she really loved my little niece, Carol. Mama told me to pack warm clothes because it was still cold up north. We get to the train station downtown about 6:30p.m.that afternoon. The train was scheduled to leave at seven o'clock. Mama road with daddy to take me to the train station she told me to be real careful and stay alert because people up north weren't as friendly as people in the south. We boarded the train and got seated; I was sitting by a window where I could see mama and daddy standing on the deck. I began to wave goodbye until I couldn't see them anymore.

We road for about 15 minutes, before the conductor came down the aisle to check everybody's ticket. As he clipped our tickets, he invites us to the dining car. Nearly everyone in my car got up and immediately went to the dining car. When we got seated a waiter came to our table. He gave us a menu and took our orders, there were lining tablecloths on every table. It was like being in a scene of an old movie. I just ordered pie and coffee that was some of the best coffee I had ever tasted in my life. All of the people I was sitting with were classmates. We talked for hours about what we expected to get from the conference. I thought it was interesting that we were going to able to meet some of the authors of our textbooks. Most everybody else just thought it was cool being away from school.

Our schedule indicated we should arrive in Chicago about 9:00 or 9:30 next morning. That was not a problem because we were probably going to be up all night anyway, playing cards and having a good time, which most of us did. About 2:00 AM everybody was getting pretty sleepy, so we went back to our seats. I was almost too excited to fall asleep but I did. When I woke up it was morning, a classmate sitting next to me was shaking my arm, and telling me it is time to wake up. It was 9:00 AM and we were come into the Chicago train terminal. I couldn't see very much mostly, all I saw was rail lines and that we were up high looking over some streets. When the train stopped, we step off to a blistering cold chilling wind. Mama was right it was still cold up north. After we got our luggage there were cabs already waiting for us. The cabs took us straight to our hotel; there were so many cars on the streets. The traffic was awful and there so many tall building; I was taking it all in. Our cabs drove to the front door of the hotel; it was some kind of beautiful. When we walked into the lobby through swinging doors it was like a picture on a postcard very plush and elegant. I had never in my life thought I would stay somewhere so grand. After we checked in and got our keys to our rooms, the bellhops brought our luggage up. They had on those cute little uniforms and hats like you saw on television or in the movies.

After my roommate and I got settled in we freshen up and rested a while, after that we were ready to explore our surrounding. The conference wasn't starting until eight o'clock the next morning that gave us time for little leisure. We eat lunch with some of our class mates and afterwards we went into the conference area to look at some of the displays, the presenters were putting up. We didn't see anything fascinating there, so we all decided to go back to our rooms and rest a while. I made a few phone calls to relatives; the only person that answered was Carolyn. It was so good to hear her voice, she seemed happy that I called. After we talked for a while she invited me to dinner, and I accepted. She told me she would pick me up at the hotel around 7:30 p.m. I asked my roommate if she wanted come with me. She told me she had made plans but she thanked me for asking her to join us.

When Carolyn picked me up, she had the biggest smile on her face. She gave me a hug, I was smiling too. It was so nice of her to

God Sent Us Angels In The Form of Good White Folks

invite me to dinner. As we entered her house there were several people there already. She introduced me and we all get along very well. Everyone started talking and asking me so many questions about Mississippi. They were asking me did I know various people, because nearly everyone there was from Jackson or other parts of Mississippi. Carolyn came to my rescue when she announced that dinner was ready to be served, and everyone took their seat at the table, that was a relief. There was one gentleman there from New York. As he began to talk with me he proceeded to ask me about something that he had heard many years ago. He said "I would like to ask you a question?" I looked over at him and smiled and I said "of course what is your question?" He said "I'm told that there is a Street in Jackson, where Jackson State College is located that is named Lynch street, because it is where the white people use to hang black people."

I took a deep breath with all that was in me, trying to not look angry. I smiled and looked at him gracefully and said, "First of all, because of much ignorance over the years, untrue rumors like that have plagued our city and state." "The fact is John R Lynch Street was named for a prominent black statesman who served in the 1800's during Reconstruction as a congressman in Mississippi and therefore, Lynch Street is not where white people or anybody lynched black people." There was total silence at the table. Carolyn being the gracious hostess she was simply said "My goodness Clem, I never even knew that." I knew he didn't know any better, but it made me angry that people from Mississippi didn't know enough about our state's history to come to the defense of our state, or be ashamed of where they came from. The fact that people who had never been to our state would take such a negative attitude about our people in our state from just hearsay. The fact is I didn't see where the majority of black people in Chicago were living any better than the black people in Mississippi. As Carolyn was driving to her house, it seemed to me that all the houses were extremely too close to each other, and the area that she drove through to get to her house, were huge apartment complexes that looked dilapidated, which they called "*the projects."* They were not the best housing I had seen, and I certainly didn't desire to live there, but I didn't say anything impolite to hurt anyone's feelings about those houses or projects. I knew that that was just one part of their inner-city. There are some good and some bad areas in all cities.

The rest of the evening went fine and everyone was in a joyful mood. We laughed and talked and played cards for a while, but it was time for me to go because I had my early morning conference to attend. I told everyone how nice it was to meet them, and said my good-byes. As Carolyn drove me back to the hotel, she said she thought we really had a wonderful visit. I told her how much I appreciated her hospitality, and I hoped to see her again before I left. Then I told her I hope I didn't insult her friend that was at the dinner. She assured me that everything was alright and that everybody there had a good time. She also told me that it was quite refreshing because the young man that was there was so arrogant. She was happy that it turned out that way, because he was one of the people in their group that always had negative things to say about Mississippi. She said, "Maybe that would shut him up for while," we both laughed. I was so thankful that it turn out that way, because I wouldn't want to do anything to embarrass Carolyn with her friends.

When I got back to the hotel some of my classmates was sitting in the lounge area. There was a jazz group playing music that was sounding really good. My roommate was sitting with them, so I joined them for while. Everyone asked me how was the dinner party. I told it was very nice, but I didn't go into any details. I just left it at that. I set and enjoyed the music with them for about an hour and then I left. When I got to the room, I guess I didn't know how tired I was. By the time I got dressed for bed and l laid down; I went to sleep as soon as my head hit the pillow.

My roommate was up bright and early. She was making so much noise it woke me up. She saw me awake and asked me "did I wake you?" I told her "yes, but that's okay I needed to get up anyway." We got downstairs just in time for breakfast. Our classmates were already there along with our professors. After breakfast we went immediately into the conference room. We broke out into groups and went to different sessions. We all met again around twelve o'clock for lunch. We had a lot of good discussions at the lunch table about different psychological concepts as we critique the presenter. Most of them had done an excellent job of describing their discipline and the advances that had been made in psychology.

From the feedback at the lunch table, we were all getting a lot from the conference. By the end of the day we were all tired and just wanted to relax a while. Our instructors wanted us to meet them for short time to discuss the next day's activities. We all agreed to meet for dinner in the hotel restaurant. While we were at dinner, Mrs. B. Mosley assigned us our new arrangement for the next day's sessions that she wanted us to attend. She wanted to make sure that we all shared in the different sessions to gain more knowledge. After she finished, she told us that we were on our own for the rest of the evening.

One of our classmates told us he had met a person in the hotel that invited us to an actor's cast party on one of the upper floors of the hotel. He said the person was in the cast of the musical stage play that was in town. That sounded like fun. A party was just fine with me. Naturally the girls wanted to go freshen up and re-dress for the party. That was fine with the guys, so everybody agreed to meet after we re-dressed. It took about an hour for us to get ready.

We were dressed and ready to go to the party. We all met at the elevator and went to the upper floor where the party was. When we went in the large room it was so smoky you could cut the smoke with a knife. The aroma in the room was very unpleasant to me. I was holding on close to John, my classmate. I asked him "what in the world is that odor?" He leaned over and whispered in my ear and said" smells like pot to me." They were playing Jimmy Hendrix on the stereo. The music was loud, psychedelic lights were flashing. As we move closer to the center of the room there was a group of long haired individuals (Hippies), both male and female sitting Indian style on the floor around this big bowl that looked like it was full of grass. They were passing around what looked like large cigarettes to each other. John said "now I am *sure* it's pot, we smell." He leaned over again and whispered in my ear, "I told you it was pot." You can imagine me being a young woman from the Deep South, never experiencing nothing more than a wine cooler as a drug. Of course I had heard of marijuana but I had never seen or smelled it before. I had seen movies and television shows with scenes like this many times, but never in my wildest imagination would I believe I would be caught in this position.

The fear that came over me was overwhelming. I held tighter to John's arm, as I whispered to him, "I have got to get out of here. " I felt a heat wave coming over me. I started sweating and perspiring too... as I started backing up trying to find the doorknob. As we navigated our way to the door, all I could think of was, "we are going to get arrested." I began to pray silently, "Lord please don't let us get arrested in Chicago, you know we are innocent, we didn't know all this was going on." I was one thankful soul when we get outside that door. I guess you know that was enough excitement for me that night. I didn't know where the rest of our classmates were, who had gone to party with us, but I knew one thing for sure, I was not going back in there to see.

When I got back to my room my roommate was already there. I asked her how long she had been back in the room. She said that her eyes started to burn at the party and she had to leave because her tears were clouding her vision. I said to her "that was absolutely too much smoke wasn't it." She said "man it was awful, I thought I was going blind." I told her "I don't know what was the worst, the smoke or the smell." My clothes smelled awful and so did my hair. I had to shower to get the odor off of my skin and hair. That was an experience, I just couldn't figure out why anyone would want to smoke something that smells so bad. It was sort of like being in a barn with cow manure burning. That's the only thing I could equate it to.

God Sent Us Angels In The Form of Good White Folks

By the last day of the conference, we all had many memorable experiences. We had gained a wealth of knowledge, met in person some of our favorite textbook writers, and had experienced psychological growth and development. It was time for us to pack up and get back on the train, for our ride back home. I think our teachers were very proud of the way we had responded to the conference. The experience was truly a blessing to me. I was so appreciative of that opportunity. I wondered if any of the other students felt the same. By the time that thought had ended, my roommate came up to me and said, "This was really a wonderful experience." I simply responded, "Indeed it was." I barely had time to call Carolyn to tell her I was getting ready to leave. I had been so busy with the rest of the conference until I didn't get a chance to do anymore visiting. I called a few of the relatives on mama's call list and simply spoke with them to apologize for not getting an opportunity to visit with them.

All of them assured me that they understood, and they wanted me to give their love to all of the folks back home. My mother's aunt Martha told me to tell mama that she was going to come down to Mississippi to visit soon. I assured her that I would give mama the message and said my good-byes. As I began to pack, I did feel sorry that I didn't get a chance to meet the other relatives, but I only had three days.

When we were riding to the train station, I was looking at the congested traffic on the streets. I was glad that our streets in Jackson weren't like that. I guess big city living takes a little getting used to, but I was happy that I wasn't going to be the one having to get used to it. There was so much to be happy about living in a small city. I had always loved Jackson, and I think my visit to Chicago made me love and appreciate Jackson all the more. When I got on the train and got seated, as we slowly moved out of the train terminal, I was looking out the window. A wonderful sense of peace came over me as we slowly moved out of the city. I looked around at all the tall buildings, the projects and the houses so close together. I was very thankful that I was from a small city in Mississippi.

The ride back home seemed shorter, as traveling goes. When we arrived home, it was such a good feeling. Daddy was there right on time. I was so happy to see him, he was all smiles. He asked me how my trip was. I told him I had lots to tell. "It was wonderful, I liked Chicago all right, but I would not like to live there. "First of all it was freezing cold, and the wind almost blows you away. "The houses in the city were much too close and I hated the part of the city they called "the projects." Daddy laughed and said "you didn't see it all, don't be so quick to judge, you may go there one day and like it. "

When we got home mama was sitting in the living room drinking a cup of coffee. She and daddy both loved their coffee. She said. "Well, how did you like the big city?" I told her it was okay, but I didn't think I would like to live there." She asks me why, and I told her the same thing I had told daddy. "It was too cold, the winds almost blow you away, the houses were too close and the building where people lived that was called "the projects" were awful. I was tired, so I just sat down in the living room for a while. I told mama that I did get to see Carolyn and Carol, and I had dinner with her. But I did get a chance to see Aunt Martha or any of the other relatives. I told her when I called the other numbers she had given me no one answer.

She said that was okay, Aunt Martha had called her and told her that she had talked with me. Mama said "well, everybody else must've been at work." and she left it at that. I told mama about what a nice experience I had at the conference, but I didn't tell her anything about the party or what went on. I know mama would have had a fit (been very upset), just the thought of drugs made her nervous.

For the rest of the weekend the thoughts of the experiences I had at the conference kept replaying in my mind. I had truly had a wonderful time and again in I was so very thankful. Because every experience I had was a spin off from my mother's Good White Folks Angels compassion.

God Sent Us Angels In The Form of Good White Folks

Spring break was over and I was back at school. It was time to get back to work. When I got on campus I was really tired I had been working on several turned papers. I was sitting in the Student Union Building one morning extremely sleepy from pulling an all nighters studying. When what to my wondering eyes did appear a tall handsome young man. Who somehow caught my eye and for no apparent reason, came over to the table where I was sitting. He spoke politely and asked, if he could buy me a cup of coffee. Knowing, that I needed coffee more than anything at that moment my response was "yes, thank you" then he asked me how did I take my coffee, and my response was "kind of like you brown and sweet." I can tell you right now that was the height of my flirting. I was just glad to get a free cup of coffee. By the time he got back with my coffee, my closest friend at that time Sandra Grimes had sat down to join me. He introduced himself and after our casual introductions, he asked Sandra if she wanted a cup coffee. Sandra said "why yes thank you." He immediately got up from the table and went and got her coffee.

We laughed and talked for while and it was time for us to go to class. We both thanked Calvin for the coffee he had brought us. Out of nowhere I looked at Sam and announced to her "he's going to be my husband." We both started to laugh and went on to class. After class I ran into Calvin outside of the Student Union building and we started to talk. He told me he had just spent a tour of duty in Vietnam, and was attending school on the G.I. Bill. We talked a bit about his travels. I wanted to know everything about over there. As we were talking my best male friend I had on Jackson State's campus, Earl Hendricks came up and begins to talk to me. Calvin thought Earl was my boyfriend, I could tell by the way he responded to Earl's greeting. Earl put his arm around my shoulders and said "Rabbit" which was his nickname for me. "What time is your last class?" "I answered 2:00 o'clock" I just wanted you to look over a paper I wrote." I told him that I would meet him back at Student Union building after class. I introduced Calvin to Earl and explained to Calvin that Earl was my best male friend at school. We always had coffee in the morning and studied together. I could see that Calvin appeared to be relieved. He had a slight smile on his face and became a bit friendlier with Earl.

I told Earl, Calvin was a Vietnam vet like he was, and you would've thought that I had lit a fire in the fireplace, boy did they began to talk. They had a lot in common and an instant friendship ignited. Well after about a 10 minute Vietnam reminiscent session between Calvin and Earl, I made my excuses and left and went to class. As I wave goodbye and a quick look back, I could see that they were still talking and that was okay.

After my class was over I went back to the student union building. Earl was waiting in the Grill, he had his turn paper with him, as we begin to look over his work, Calvin walked in and came over and sat with us. There was a fair skin young lady setting over at a table not too far from us. Earl losing focus on his paper mentioned to me that he sure would like to meet her. I told him when we finish reviewing your paper I'll go over and ask her to join us. He said okay and we finish checking his paper. I went over to the table where the young lady was sitting, introduce myself and told her that it was a young man at our table that wanted to meet her. She had told me that her name was Ruby. She thanked me and said that she did not have time to come over because her next class was in a few minutes, and she did not want to be late. I told her I understood and I went back to our table.

Earl seemed disappointed when I told him what she had said, but he understood. As time would have it, I had to get to work and again I bid Calvin and Earl farewell and to worker went. I had a pretty easy day that day because I was getting ready for graduation. After work I went over to the Education Department to meet with my advisor Dr. Cleopatra Thompson she had some papers and forms that she wanted me to verify, and to go over with me about my credit hours so I would be ready for graduation. It seemed that everything was in order. All I needed was 12 hours for practice teaching and take the National Teachers Exam. All was well; boy what a relief that was wonderful news to me.

God Sent Us Angels In The Form of Good White Folks

It had been two weeks and May was approaching, Calvin had asked me to go on a date. He invited me to the James Brown concert that was going to be Saturday evening, at the Coliseum. I had never been to a concert before. I really didn't like loud noises or smokey rooms, for that reason I didn't know how I would do at a concert. That Friday afternoon, Calvin asked me again about the concert and I agreed to go with him. I gave him my phone number and my address. He said he would pick me up at 6:30p.m. The concert started at 8:00pm and he wanted us to get good seats. That was fine with me; I was getting a little excited. I liked James Brown's music and the way he danced on stage.

When Saturday came, Calvin called to tell me that his sister was coming to the concert with us. That was fine, because I remembered his sister from Brinkley; we had a few classes together. As a matter of fact I knew they were twins. I had told my parents that my date was a nice young man from school, and that he had asked me to go to a concert with him. When Calvin and his sister came, my mother answered the door. They both were dressed like hippies, with Indian style bandannas around their head and suede fringed vests, I was a little choked up myself. I knew that mama was not going to like the way they were dressed. My mother immediately called me to the back and sternly asked me had I lost my mind. While we were in the back talking, Calvin and his sister started playing the piano in the living room that Mrs. Cole had given me and singing, "His Eyes Are On The Sparrow," one of daddy's favorite hymns. That singing won daddy over. He was smiling and singing along with my date and his sister.

Daddy came in the room where my mother and I were. I was surprised when daddy said "Rosella, they seem to be okay." Daddy was taken by the fact that at least they knew a church song. Mama gave in, but I could tell she didn't like it one bit. Daddy liked that church hymn alright, but he still told Calvin what time to have me back home. If you were age 18 or 40, the time was still the same, 12:00 o'clock. I was a little embarrassed actually, but I tried to play it off, after all I was 21 years old. The fact is it didn't matter how old you were, if you were living in your parent's home you had to abide by their rules. As the Bible says: (Honor Thy Father and Mother; which is the first Commandment with Promise; that it may be well with thee, and thou mayest live long on the earth) *EPHESIANS* **6:1-3**

Our choice was to obey or get your own house. Of course not being gainfully employed my choice was to stay at home until I could get a job. Living at home wasn't bad; we had nutritious food, shelter and clothing every need met.

We got to the concert at a good time; I didn't want to set to close to the front because I knew the music would be to be loud. So we settled for seats in the middle rows, several groups came out to perform before James Brown appeared. The performances were really very good but the smoke was awful and the crowd screaming along with the loud music gave me a bit of a head ache. I must say over all I did enjoy the concert. James Brown's performance was excellent however; I did get teary-eyed because of the smoke.

After the concert we went to the little lounge just off of Livingston Road to get a bite eat. The lounge had a nice dance floor, when Calvin asked me to dance the jukebox was playing, "Mama I Think I've Found That Girl" by the Jackson five. I must say as he held me dancing it was a nice feeling. I think at that moment is when I believed I was actually falling in love. I wasn't really ready to go but after that dance, Calvin told me it was time for us to leave, because he didn't want to upset my father. The fact that he respected my father's wishes made me admired him that much more.

When I got home, Calvin walked me to the door. Just as he was going to give me a little kiss on the jaw, daddy flicked the porch light on and he ended up giving me a hand shake as he said goodbye. When I walked in, mama was still up. She started questioning me about who my date was. She didn't forget to mention that she didn't like the way he was dressed. She said "I just can't see what you see in that tennis shoe wearing boy." I said to her "it was just a date; it is not as if I'm going to marry him or anything." Then I heard mama say under her breath "I surely hope not."

To keep the peace at home, I didn't do much mentioning Calvin when I was home. I had so much on my mind to get ready for graduation, until I just got back into my classes studying and trying to keep my average up. However, Calvin and I were still having coffee in the mornings before I went to class. Most afternoons we met at the end of class and set around and talked. I must say we were growing closer and he had started talking about marriage, even to the point of how many children he would like to have. I admit that I was getting a little taken with how mature and intelligent he was.

It was mid May a beautiful spring day; Calvin and I met and begin to talk about a party that Earl was going to have. He wanted to make sure that I was going to be able to attend the party with him. I told him I would meet him at the party because Ruby and I were coming together. He said that would be fine as long as I was going be there. After that I told him that I had to go home to get ready for work. I was going to baby sat for the Yelvertons that evening and I didn't want to be late. I caught the evening number eight bus going back to New Port Street. When I got home I had a few minutes before it was time to go to work. Daddy was watching the evening news, which was just about over. Mama had dinner ready so I ate a bite. After that I just rested before time for Mr. Yelverton to pick me up. I had finished resting just in time as Mr. Yelverton drove up. I was tired, but didn't mind making a little extra money. When I got to their house, the children were already in bed, so I really didn't have anything to do. There wasn't even a dish in the sink. I watched TV for a while, and afterwards I got one of my books and started to study. I would check every now and then on the children to make sure that they were under the covers because it was chilly in the house to me. All was well. The Yelvertons were back in about four hours. Mr. Yelverton ask me how was school as Ms Ann went to the back while we were talking. She soon returned with $20, which was my pay for the evening.

That was wonderful. Mr. Yelverton seemed very pleased that I was doing well in school, and that I was just about to finish. On the ride home Mr. Yelverton asked me had I decided what I wanted to do when I graduated from school, I said, "I probably will teach a while." He just smiled and said "that sounds good. Let me know." and I said "yes sir."

When I got home I was very sleepy and tired. I went straight to bed. The next morning daddy and mama were listening to the morning news. There had been a student protest and rioting on Jackson State's campus. The news reported that about 9:30 PM, students on campus started fires and overturned vehicles. Firefighters that came on the scene requested the police to come. Almost 100 Jackson police and the Mississippi Highway Patrol tried to control the crowd as firefighters extinguished the fire. When firefighters left the scene a little before midnight, police tried to disperse the crowd that had gathered in front of Alexander Hall.

About 12:00 AM, officers opened fire on the students in front of the dormitory. At least 140 shots were said to have been fired by some 40 Highway patrolman, using shotguns at about 30 to 50 feet. They shot up nearly every window in the dormitory building facing J. R. Lynch Street, according to the National News Reports that came out days after the incident. Daddy told me that the school was closed. We didn't have to attain class that day because several students had gotten killed and some wounded. Daddy again said the shooting took place at Alexander Hall, the girl's dormitory. A knot came in my stomach because that's where my friend (Sam), Sandra Grimes lived. Mama said "this is awful. When are they going to stop shooting the children down like animals?" It had only been 10 days since four student protesters had been shot and killed at Kent State University in Ohio.

A male Jackson State student, Phillip Lafayette Gibbs, 21, a father with a young son, and a Jim Hill High School student James Earl Green, 17, a senior were killed. Twelve other students were injured by flying glass and buck shots.

Daddy said, "Lord help us all. This is just too much when children can't even go to school in peace." As daddy was talking the phone rang, it was Mrs. Cole. Mama answered. All of her phone conversation, she just kept saying, "no ma'am." When she got off the phone she told us it was Mrs. Cole. She was asking her was I on campus during the unrest. She was just checking to see if I was alright. Mama said Mrs. Cole told her "Rosie, I just don't know what's going on. We all have just got to pray that this killing will stop." I was having the same terrible feeling I had when I heard of the assassinations of Dr. King, President, Kennedy, Meager Evers and all the other deaths that had taken place, locally and nationwide. It was just a sick feeling all over, an emptied choked up feeling that is the only way to describe it. I was dreading going back on campus, but I had no choice. I had to go back. After all, it was a blessing that I was just about to graduate. I just couldn't give up now. I had indeed come too far from where I had started from.

As time passed we were allowed back on campus. There was a sadness about campus. The sight of the remnant of all the devastation that had happened on campus was everywhere. As we put what happened in one of the four corners of our minds, we tried to continue class as usual. That was still English competency test to take and practice teaching internships to complete. And as I was getting those things done, Calvin and I continued our courtship. By the time July came, he had indeed proposed marriage to me. I was not surprised by his proposal, but I was unnerved, to say the least, in how I was going to break the news to my mother. As I kept putting him off, he was getting rather impatient. I was going to be finished with school soon and I think he thought I was going to leave him behind.

With no warning, unannounced to me, the first week in July, Calvin bravely came to our house, and while sitting on the front porch with daddy, he asked daddy for my hand in marriage. I nearly choked to death on the glass of tea I was drinking. As daddy smiled, he called mama to come to the front porch. Knowing that mama had not taken to Calvin as daddy had, I thought she might have a seizure and die right there on the porch. God gave Calvin mercy that day, because mama simply looked at daddy and said. "What do you think about it?" Daddy said smiling, "its fine by me." At that very moment Calvin took out a jewelry box with a ring in it and slipped it on my finger. He looked at me smiling and said, "For the third time will you marry me? I said "for the first time yes, I'll marry you." Mama looked at us both and she just said "oh well," and she went in the house. I left daddy and Calvin on the porch talking, and went in the house to check on mama. I could tell that mama wasn't pleased, but she didn't say anything. I didn't know if that was good or bad. I figure when Mama got to know Calvin better she would be alright. I know she just wanted the best for me, and that would have been a man with a job and money, not going to school on the G.I. Bill. But it was what it was. Calvin and I decided on a small private ceremony, something simple because we didn't have any money.

Everyone was very sweet to us. He was the only boy in his family and his sisters adored him. All of his sisters seemed to like me as well, and so did his mother. He and his twin sister were the youngest children of the family, but he didn't seem to be spoiled at all. For someone in their early 20s, I thought he was quite mature. School was out and I finished my coursework and that was a plus. I had accepted a teaching position with Westside Elementary School in the Hinds County school district. That was encouraging because at least we would have some money coming in. Mama was still having a problem with the fact that Calvin didn't have a job. I know what mama was thinking, but when you are young and in love, most times you are not thinking on your parent's level.

When mama told Mr. Yelverton I was getting married, he asked mama what did I need. She said most everything, Mr. Yelverton told mama, "Tell Clem to call me." When I called him, he asked me what did I want for a wedding present and I told him, "Whatever God lay on your heart will be fine." The next week when mama went to work, Mr. Yelverton and Ms. Ann gave mama an envelope and told her to give it to me. They told her it was my wedding present from them. When I opened the envelope, there was a card with a check in it. The card read, "We thank you so much for all the years you have helped with our children. We hope that this token will help you have a wonderful wedding." There was enough money in there to buy me a beautiful wedding gown, to pay for all the reception, and there was a voucher in there for six-months of rent to the newly built Mayes Street apartment. I was so happy that all I could do was cry. When I picked up the phone and called Mr. Yelverton I was still crying. When he answered I was all choked up. I told him how much I appreciated what he and Ms. Ann had done for me. He simply said "Clementine, you know Rosie is family, we love you all, and would do anything to help you." I thanked him again, smiling and sobbing at the same time.

Calvin and I were married August 1970, at my sister's home, in a beautiful ceremony with family and close friends attending. Mama used all the talent that she had acquired for garnishing beautiful food trays, and decorating tables. She also used her talent for preparing gourmet cuisine that she had learned to make my reception food tables look exquisite. I was so happy. God just kept on blessing me through my mother's "Good White Folks Angels."

Hard Times and Heartaches

Several years later I stopped by my mama's house one evening. Mama was so upset. She had learned that Mrs. Buford's house had caught fire and was completely destroyed. Mrs. Buford was not home when the fire occurred. There was no loss of life, but she didn't have anything saved. The house was a total loss. She stayed with Ms Ann and Mr. Gene while everything was being handled by her insurance company.

A few months after the fire, Mrs. Buford's insurance paid off. She found a house off Old Canton Road on Kaywood Circle. Of course Mama helped her move in. Mama said that the new house was better for Mrs. Buford. The stairs in the old house were getting to be too much for both of them. Mama was still helping Mrs. Buford on an as-needed basis. Both mama and Mrs. Buford's health was declining. Most of the time when mama went to Mrs. Buford's, Ms Ann or one of Mrs. Buford's other daughters would be there to help out. They knew Mama was getting older and she couldn't do much work because of her arthritis. For that reason mama only worked a few days a week and on holidays. She was mostly working for the Baileys and the Yelvertons. Tot just wanted mama to be at her house, because she just enjoyed having her mother Rosie around.

A short time after Mama got Mrs. Buford settled in, Mama had another family emergency. One morning mama had gone to work

God Sent Us Angels In The Form of Good White Folks

at the Yelvertons. When she went in, Mr. Gene was sitting at the table still in his pjs and robe with his face in his hands. Mama knew something was wrong. Mr. Yelverton was always dressed before mama got to work. She spoke to him and asked him if he was feeling alright. He said "Well, Rosie, I'll tell you things have been better." Mama told him "As good a man as you are, God is not going to let anything too bad happen to you. God will make it alright, don't worry." Mr. Gene told her, "Thank you, Rosie, I needed that," he had his coffee and went and got dressed. A few months later the Yelvertons moved and Mama was right there helping them.

They moved to a townhouse off Ridgewood Road. Mama said Miss Ann told her, "Rosie, if you see something you want just put it aside. I don't have room for too many things." Mama told her, "Baby, I don't want a thing," but Miss Ann got a big box and started putting household items in it. Mama thought she was packing the box to take to her new house. At the end of the day, when they had finished, the movers came, and after they loaded the moving van, the big box was still sitting on the kitchen floor. Mama told Miss Ann "the movers have forgotten this box." Miss Ann came over to mama and started to cry. She fell into Mama's arms and said, "No, Rosie, that box is for you. I want you to have those things. I love you and I thank you for being here with me. I couldn't have done this without you." So there they were, both of them, just standing there hugging and crying in the middle of the kitchen. Mama, Mr. Gene and Miss Ann were already very close, but they were even closer after that. Mama was truly a loving faithful force in their lives. She just kept spreading and sharing her love in their family.

A few years after that, when the 1979 flood hit Jackson, nearly all the homes in northeast Jackson were flooded, including downtown. Tragedy yet again hit the Yelvertons. Their townhouse was flooded and they lost everything they had. Of course, Mr. Gene called Mama to tell her what had happened. When Mama got the news that morning, she could not believe it. She sat in the very chair Mr. Gene had given her, the chair that sat by her stack of Bibles, books from Billy Graham, and Daily Bread devotionals from Mrs. Cole, and she started to cry.

Mama said, "It just seems like the devil is on their trail. Because they are so good, he just won't leave them alone." (Speaking of the devil) "I just don't understand." She started to pray, "Lord, please help them, help my children, please, Lord." Mr. Gene had told Mama not to worry before he hung up. That didn't do any good. She was just sick. "You can't keep a good man down and he is a good man," she said holding her Bible. God heard and answered mama's prayer for the Yelvertons.

Everything worked out for the good. It took a while, but the Yelvertons bounced back, and Mama was right there to help them get moved into their new home. Mr. Gene, Miss Ann and Mama continued to cook and have many years of family memories. Mama worked for her *"Good White Folks Angels"* for over 40 years. She saw generations come and go. She was there for every joy, every heartache and pain.

Mrs. Buford, Mrs. Cole, Miss Ann and Mr. Gene Yelverton preceded Mama in death, yet they lived on in her heart. As mama grew older and dementia set in, as I was bringing her home from the doctor one day, she insisted that I take her to see Mrs. Cole. At that time Mrs. Cole had been dead several years. She cried when I told her Mrs. Cole was not there anymore. When I got her home I had to call Mobile to let her talk to Little Jane, (Mrs. Jane Potts), before she would settle down. Little Jane told her "Rosie, mother is no longer with us, but I know she still loves you, and I love you to." Mama said, "Yes, ma'am I Love You Too," and she stopped crying. Even with the onset of dementia, mama still remembered who was good to her. (True love last)

She spoke of her "White Folks Angels" often with much joy in her heart. She had found her niche in life, caring for her own children and her husband of sixty-seven years, as well as her "Good White Folks Angels" and their children. Mrs. Cole gave Mama financial support until she died, and when Mrs. Cole passed in 1997, Mrs. Jane

God Sent Us Angels In The Form of Good White Folks

Potts, (Little Jane), who now lives in Mobile Alabama, continued financial support until Mama's death, still proclaiming, "Rosie was like a mother to me."

As mama aged, she would go to work at Mrs. Tot Bailey's. Tot would not let her work. She would sit Mama down and serve her. My mother received many gifts, which included money from her "Good White Angels," but more than anything she treasured their love. Mama attended many family gatherings in the Bailey's home as an honored family member. Tot and Sissy still speak lovingly of their Mother Rosie. She got to receive love and appreciation from the white children she had helped rise while she lived. Tot, Sissy and I were together not too long ago as we reminisced about mama and Mrs. Buford and the rest of the family. We had a wonderful time. It was as if we were all girls again. We were sharing different stories. Sissy told of the time Mrs. Buford came to Texas to visit her and it was time for her to leave, because Sissy had to go back to work. Sissy told us that when she got her mother to the air port, Mrs. Buford passed out. Right there on the air port floor. Sissy said that she was so embarrassed that she almost passed out herself. Sissy said she got down on her knees and whispered in her mother's ear, *"mother if you don't get up right now. I am going to call an ambulance to come take you to the hospital."* She said her mother got up and got on that plane, fast. We spent hours talking and laughing, until tears literally streamed down our faces. There was never a dull moment. Of course I had to tell of many of the exciting times mama and Mrs. Buford had, as well as Jimmy and the rest of the family. I will never forget the wonderful experiences we are still having. I think my mother, Mrs. Buford, Mr. Yelverton, Mrs. Cole and the rest of the family would be proud that we are still in contact with each other. And the love and respect is still there.

The day I learned Mr. Gene Yelverton Jr. had died. Mama was in the hospital. I was sitting with her and read of his death in a newspaper. I didn't tell Mama. I always wanted to be able to care for him when he aged, but it must not have been meant to be. I cried a long time that day.

Mama died in February 2008, at the age of 87, in my home, with all of her children and grand children at her bed side. God blessed me to be able to care for her. It was a childhood prayer of mine, to be able to care for my parents in their old age.

> I found this bookmark in Mamas things. She kept it for her would be like to keep & think of here & had each love. Little Jane your billed her beautiful you use it.

> You've given friendship meaning in a way that's all your own. With the special gifts and talents that belong to you alone. And I know that of the blessings I could hope for life to send, None could make me happier than knowing you're my friend.
>
> HAPPY MOTHER'S DAY
> Rosie — Happy Mothers Day! I hope this will help you to go and get your Teeth fixed!!! Love, Jane (Cole) Potts

If The Truth Be Told

Many people, white and black, migrated to the north, east and west, from Mississippi in the early years. Sometimes some of them took a good Mississippi education with them. Some of them came back when the fight was nearly over, to reap the benefits of the new south, or to exploit the past, for whatever reason. I do know that Mississippi has experienced a profound change. We have integrated churches, (I know because I am a member of one) organizations, work places and recreational facilities. I for one would not live anywhere else. I have been to the north, south, east, and west, and can make that choice based on what I saw and experienced when I went to other cities and states.

We thank God for organizations such as Mission Mississippi, founded by Dr. Dolphus Weary, President to promote unity in the body of Christ across racial and denomination lines. The institute For Racial Reconciliation, founded by our 58th Governor of the State of Mississippi, Honorable Governor William Winter, First Presbyterian, First Baptist, Galloway United Methodist, Living Waters Bible Fellowship Church, New Horizon and many other churches and groups working together to mend, build, and strengthen race relations in the City of Jackson, and the entire State of Mississippi. I will not be a hypocrite and say that we have no racial problems, but I can truly say that "**A *Change Has Come.*"** I have tried to show the other side of the coin, of race relations that happened in the fifties, sixties and until present day, between blacks and whites, and some of the good things that are happening in Jackson and Mississippi as a whole today. I was twelve years old when James Meredith integrated the University of Mississippi in Oxford. That was fifty years ago. Two years ago I sat at my granddaughter's graduation from the University Mississippi School of Law. "Glory be to God." I would like to recommend the reading of the book, "AN AMERICAN INSURRECTION," (The Battle of Oxford, Mississippi, 1962), by William Doyle, to get a true and accurate account of what really happened in Mississippi during that time. It will let the reader of this book understand just what a miracle this book has shown.

I feel deep in my heart, that there are many people of all different races that have had similar experiences as my mother and I had. But for some reason, these stories are not told. It seems that people love the horror stories of the Deep South, especially Mississippi, God knows there are many. However, God also knows that there has been many wonderful stories of good, kind and loving relationships that people of different races had in the south.

My hope is that when people think of Mississippi from this day forward that they think about the "Mississippi Love Story" shown in this book between the races.

"Man Of Honor

The Honorable Governor William F. Winter is the 58th Governor of the State of Mississippi from 1980-1984; a strong man of faith he has been for many years an advocate of equal education for all children in the state of Mississippi and is credited with the passage of the Mississippi Education Reform Act. He is hailed as the Father of Racial Reconciliation in the state in which The William Winter Institute for Racial Reconciliation has been established on the campus of the University of Mississippi, Oxford. He is a graduate of the University Of Mississippi Law School. He is a World War II veteran and has held the offices of Mississippi State House of Representative, State Treasurer, Lieutenant Governor and Governor; he is a published author of the book, The Measure of Our Days; Writings of William F. Winter published by University Press, Jackson. Governor Winter was a member of President's Clinton's Advisory Board on Race 1997-1998, in 2008 he received the Profile in Courage Award by the John F. Kennedy Presidential Library and Museum for his work in the advancement of education and racial reconciliation. He is still a practicing attorney with Watkins Ludlam Winter & Stennis Law Firm based in Jackson, Mississippi.

Giving Back

Some of the proceeds from the sale of this book will be used to Administrator The Eugene Yelverton Jr. Scholarship Fund, through Renaissance Foundation, Inc., a non-profit organization set up to help children further their education, that I may pay it forward for what Mr. Eugene Yelverton Jr. did for me, a little colored girl in Jackson, Mississippi.

One of Mrs. Tot Bailey's and Mama's greatest dreams was to write a cook book together, to honor those dreams; I have included some of the recipes they loved to cook together.

Thanks Be To God.

From Tot's and Mama's Cookbook

Mr. Gene Yelvertons

Grit Soufflé

1 cup grated cheese
3egg yokes beaten until thick
3 eggs whites beaten, until stiff
1 teaspoon salt
½ teaspoon black pepper
½ cup cooked grits
½ stick margarine or butter
Blend cheese, egg yolks, salt and margarine into grits.
Spread beaten egg whites onto top of soufflé, bake until golden brown.
Handle with care to keep top from falling

Eggplant Casserole

1 eggplant
4 cups dry bread crumbs
1 slightly beaten egg mixed with
½ cup water
Oil for frying
1 chopped onion
½ chopped green pepper
½ stick of butter or margarine
2 ½ cups canned or fresh tomatoes
1 teaspoon salt
1/8 teaspoon pepper
1 teaspoon sugar
1cup sharp cheddar cheese

Peel and slice the eggplant in ¼ inch slices. Dip in bread crumbs, then in egg and milk mixture, and back in bread crumbs Fry in hot oil until brown. Sauté the onions and green pepper in butter until soft. Add tomatoes, salt, pepper, and sugar. Cook until well blended. Place the eggplant in a two casserole in altering layers with cheese and sauce, having a top layer cheese. Bake at 350 degrees.

Squash Au Gratin

2 cups cooked squash
2 tablespoons butter or margarine melted
Salt and pepper
2 eggs beaten
1 cup buttered bread crumbs
1/3 shredded cheese
Combine squash, melted butter, or margarine, seasonings, and beaten eggs.
Alternate layers of squash, bread crumbs, and cheese in 1 quart casserole; bake at 375 degrees for ten minutes.

Butternut Squash Casserole

3 cups ground butternut squash

1 cup sugar

¼ cup butter

1 cup milk

½ cup flaked coconut

Dash salt Combine all ingredients; pour into 9 inch casserole. Bake at 325 degrees for 45 minutes.

Yields 8 servings

Mayonnaise

1 egg

¼ teaspoon dry mustard

½ teaspoon salt

1 tablespoon lemon

1 cup vegetable oil

Insert steel blade knife, place egg, mustard and salt in work bowl and process 20 seconds. Pour lemon juice down feed tube process 15 seconds. Pour one cup oil down feed tube <u>very slowly</u> processing for almost 2 minutes.

Artichoke Dip

1 can water packed artichokes, drained

1 cup mayonnaise

1pkg. Good Seasons Italian Dressing Mix Insert steel knife blade and prepare mayonnaise and reserve. Chop artichoke

With steel knife blade, add mayonnaise and seasonings and blend. Chill.

Two of mama's and Mrs. Buford's favorite ingredients to cook with was nutmeg and water chestnuts. Add these two ingredients to taste.

Avocado Salad Rings

1-½ Tablespoon plain gelatin
2 Tablespoons lemon juice
¼ cup cold water
1-½ cup Mashed Avocado
1 cup boiling water
1 cup sour cream
1-¼ teaspoon salt
1 cup mayonnaise
1 teaspoon grated onion
Salad greens
Dash Tobacco Sauce
Fruits

Soften gelatin in cold water and dissolve in boiling water. Blend in salt, onion, Tobacco and lemon juice. Cool to room temperature. Cut avocado into halves and remove seeds and skin. Mash fruit, stir avocado, sour cream and mayonnaise into cooled gelatin. Place in 8in. Mold and chill until firm. Garnish with fruit, salad greens or lettuce.

Mama and Mrs. Buford would save the avocado seed, place it in water to let sprout so they could grow and avocado plant. I don't know if they had success. But you should try...

Angel Cornbread

1-½ cup cornmeal
1 cup flour
1pkg. Dry yeast
½ teaspoon soda
1 Tablespoon sugar
2 eggs
1 teaspoon salt
2 cups buttermilk
1-½ teaspoon baking powder
½ cup cooking oil

Combine dry ingredients, combine eggs, milk, and oil. Mix with dry ingredients. Bake in greased corn stick pans at 350 degrees 12-15 minutes, or bake in iron skillet or pan 15- 20 minutes.

String Bean Casserole

1 can French cut string beans
1 can mushroom soup
3 Tabs Worcestershire Sauce
1 cup cheese-cracker crumbs
4 Tabs melted butter

Drain beans, pour into baking dish, mix soup, Worcestershire sauce, and pour over beans. Top with cheese cracker crumbs, add melted butter and sprinkle paprika on top. Bake until golden brown.

Rotel Chicken

1 whole chicken or hen
2 large onions
2 large green peppers
1 stick margarine
1 (12 oz) package vermicelli or small spaghetti
1 can rotel tomatoes
1 lb. Velveeta
1 can small English peas
1 can mushrooms

Cook in salted water, enough to have 1 ½ quarts broth. Chop and sauté onions and peppers, but do not brown in margarine. Cook vermicelli or spaghetti in broth. Add rotel tomatoes and juice. Cook until thickens. Add Velveeta, chopped in large pieces. Stir until melted. Add drained peas, mushrooms, chopped chicken, onion, and pepper. Salt and pepper to taste. Pour into a large casserole dish or several small ones. Bake at 350 degrees until hot.

Party Rice

1 cup rice
½ can small mushrooms
½ teaspoon nutmeg
almonds chopped
1 can creamed mushroom soup
½ cup butter

Boil rice, rinse and season with nutmeg. Place rice in buttered casserole dish, add mushroom soup and nuts on top melt and pour ½ cup butter. Bake at 350 degrees for 20 min.

Chicken Pie

1 chicken (deboned)
2 cups broth
1 can Cream of Celery soup
1 cup self rising flour
¼ tablespoon pepper
1 stick margarine
1 cup milk

Boil chicken and take meat off bone. Line bottom of baking dish with meat. Mix 2 cups broth and 1 can of cream of Celery soup. Pour over chicken and stir well. Cook at 350 degrees until done.

From Tot's and Mama's Cook Book

Corn Pudding

2 eggs (beaten)
3 Ts melted butter
1 Table spoon sugar
1/8 t salt
1/8 t black pepper
¼ minced onion
¼ bell pepper
2 cans cream corn
T spoon flour
Mix ingredient. Bake 20 to 30 minutes at 325% to 350% until golden brown.

Asparagus Casserole

1 can asparagus
1 can peas
2 tablespoons butter
2 tablespoons flour
1 teaspoon chopped onion
1 ½ cups grated cheese
3 eggs, separated
Salt and pepper

Make cream' sauce with butter, flour, milk, and liquid from asparagus. When thick and smooth, remove from fire. Add asparagus, also drained peas, cheese and onion. Fold in beaten egg whites. Pour into buttered casserole and bake in a moderate oven 350F. About 50 minutes

★Add beaten egg yolks and blend well.

String Bean-Mushroom Casserole

1 can French cut beans
1 can mushroom soup
3 t. Worcestershire Sauce
1 cup cheese-cracker crump
4 T. melted butter (more if desired)

Drain beans, pour into baking dish. Mix soup with Worcestershire Sauce, pour over beans. Top with cheese-cracker crumbs; add melted butter and sprinkle over top paprika. Bake in hot oven until begins to brown and soup bubbles up.

Sweet Potato Pudding

4 cups cooked sweet potatoes
2 cups sugar
1 cup melted butter
3 eggs, beaten
½ teaspoon cinnamon
¼ teaspoon cloves
¼ teaspoon mace or nutmeg
½ cup milk
½ teaspoon soda

Cook sweet potatoes. Add the sugar, butter, and beaten eggs. Add the spices, then the milk in which the soda has been dissolved. Mix thoroughly and place in a greased baking dish. Bake in moderate oven- 350F. Until firm, about 1 hour.

Sweet Potato Pone

1 stick butter
1 cup sugar
¼ teaspoon salt
1 egg
¼ teaspoon cinnamon
Dash nutmeg
2 cups raw grated sweet potato
Grated rind of 1 orange
Juice of ½ orange

Melt butter; mix everything, adding potatoes last. (Blend immediately). Bake in casserole at 325 degrees for 55 minutes. Good hot or cold.

Butternut Squash Casserole

3 cups ground butternut squash

1 cup sugar

¼ cup butter

1 cup milk

½ cup flaked coconut

Dash of salt

Combine all ingredients; pour into a 9in casserole. Bake at 325 degrees for 45 minutes.

Creamy Squash Casserole

1 ½ pounds yellow squash, sliced

1 can cream of chicken soup

1 cup sour cream

1 4-ounce jar pimentos, drained and sliced

1 8 ½ ounce can sliced water chestnuts

2 medium onions, finely chopped

1 stick butter

4 ounces herbed stuffing mix

Dash of salt and pepper

Cook squash in salted water until tender (12 to 15 minutes) and drain well. Mix next 5 ingredients in a bowl. Gently fold the cooked squash into mixture. Melt ¾ stick butter in a frying pan and add stuffing mix. Add salt and pepper. Stir well. Pack most of the stuffing mix into the bottom of a 2-quart baking dish, reserving some for the topping. Pour squash mixture over stuffing and sprinkle the reserved stuffing on top. Dot rest of butter on casserole and bake at 350 degrees for 25 to 30 minutes.

Refrigerator Pickles

4 cups sugar
4 cups cider vinegar
½ cup salt
1 ¼ t. turmeric
1 ¼ t. celery seed
1 ¼ t. mustard seed
3 onions (sliced thinly) /Refrigerate at least 5 days before using. Cucumbers (sliced thinly) Mix together sugar, vinegar and spices into cold syrup. Do not heat. Wash and sterilize 4 pint jars. Stir enough cucumbers to fill jar. Stir syrup well and pour over cucumbers and onions. Screw on lids.

Pickles

1 gallon sour pickles, drained. NOT DILL
1 ½ oz. black peppercorns
1 ½ oz. Pickling spice
4 cloves garlic, finely chopped
5 lbs. sugar, minus 2 cups sugar
Slice pickles into ¼ inch rounds. Layer in gallon jar in 3 layers as follows: Pickles –sugar—spices. Ending with pickles on top. You may have to push pickles down to make them fit back into jar. Invert jar twice daily. Example, up during the day and upside down at night. Makes 8 pints.

Mock Cheese Soufflé

10 Slices white bread
3 cups milk
½ cup softened butter
1 ½ tsp. salt
1 lb. grated sharp cheddar cheese
1 tsp. dry mustard
4 eggs, slightly beaten
1 tbl. Worcestershire sauce

Remove crust from bread. Spread butter on each slice. Cut each slice into four strips. Butter a 2-quart casserole and lay alternate layers of bread strips and grated cheese, ending with grated cheese. Beat eggs well. Add seasonings and milk to eggs. Spoon egg mixture over cheese. Refrigerate for 24 hours. Bake at 350 degrees for 45 minutes.

Serves 6-8.

"*A Tough Row To Hoe*"

One of my mother's expressions to describe a difficult experience a person might be having in life was, "I have a tough row to hoe. " My mother's life was indeed a tough row to hoe, but God gave her a very sharp hoe.

Over the years God has sent me many "*Good White Folks Angels*" the list would take up many pages I would like to name just a few. Maybe in the next book I will list them all.

A Few Noted People from Mississippi According to Wikipedia

List of people from Mississippi
Activists and advocates

James Bevel (1936-2008), leader in the 1960s Civil Rights Movement, (Itta Bena)

Ruby Bridges (born 1954), first African-American child to attend an all-white school in the South, (Tylertown)

Curtis Conway "C.C." Bryant (1917–2007), African-American civil rights leader, (Tylertown) [1]

Will D. Campbell (born 1924), Baptist minister and activist, (Amite County)

James Chaney (1943–1964), African-American civil rights worker, (Meridian)

Vernon Dahmer (1908–1966), African-American civil rights leader, (Hattiesburg)

Charles Evers (born 1922), African-American civil rights leader, (Decatur)

Medgar Evers (1925–1963), African-American civil rights leader, (Decatur)

Myrlie Evers-Williams (born 1933), African-American civil rights leader, (Vicksburg)

Dianna Freelon-Foster, African-American civil rights activist, Member of the Mississippi Civil Rights Education Commission, first female and first African-American mayor of her hometown (Grenada) [2]

C. L. Franklin (1915–1984), Baptist minister and father of Aretha Franklin, (Shelby)

Duncan M. Gray, Jr. (born 1926), Episcopal clergyman, civil rights activist, (Canton)

Percy Greene (1897–1977), journalist, activist, (Jackson)

Lawrence Guyot (born 1939), civil rights activist, (Pass Christian)

Fannie Lou Hamer (1917–1977), American voting rights activist, Civil rights leader, (Ruleville)

Winson Hudson (1916–2004), civil rights activist, (Harmony)

Clyde Kennard (1927–1963), civil rights activist, (Hattiesburg)

Ed King, civil rights activist, Tougaloo chaplain, (Jackson) [3]

James Meredith (born 1933), first African-American student at the University of Mississippi, (Kosciusko)

Anne Moody (born 1940), civil rights activist, (Centreville)

Ida B. Wells-Barnett (1862–1931), civil rights activist, Women's rights activist, (Holly Springs)

Donald Wildmon (born 1938), founder and chairman of the American Family Association

Actors/Actresses

Joey Lauren Adams (born 1968), (Oxford)
Joshua Alba (born 1982), (Biloxi)
Mary Alice (born 1941), (Indianola)
Dana Andrews (1909–1992), (Covington County)
Roscoe Ates (1895–1962), (Grange)

Katherine Bailess (born 1980), film and television actress (Vicksburg)
Laura Bailey (born 1981), voice actress, (Biloxi)
Earl W. Bascom (1906-1995), film and television (Columbia)
Willie Best (1916–1962), (Sunflower)
Jimmy Boyd (1939–2009), (McComb)
Don Briscoe (1940–2004), soap opera actor, (Yalobusha County)
Geneva Carr (born 1971), television and stage actress, (Jackson)
Finn Carter (born 1960), (Greenville)
Wally Cassell (born 1915), film and television actor
Lacey Chabert (born 1982), (Purvis)
Wyatt Emory Cooper (1927–1978), Broadway actor, (Quitman)
Cassi Davis (born 1964), (Holly Springs)
Jason Dottley (born 1980), actor in Sordid Lives stage production and Logo television series, (Florence) [4]
John Dye (born 1963), (Amory)
Mary Elizabeth Ellis, television and film actress, (Laurel)
Ruth Ford (born 1915), stage and film actress, (Hazlehurst)
Morgan Freeman (born 1937), (Greenwood)
M. C. Gainey (born 1948), film and television actor, (Jackson)
Cynthia Geary (born 1965), (Jackson)
Allie Grant (born 1994), (Tupelo)
Gary Grubbs (born 1949), (Amory)
Lynn Hamilton (born 1930), (Yazoo City)
Temeceka Harris (born 1975), one-time actress, (Mound Bayou)
Beth Henley (born 1952), dramatist and actress, (Jackson)
Jim Henson (1936–1990), creator of The Muppets, (Leland)
Anthony Herrera (born 1944), (Wiggins)
Wilbur Higby (1867–1934), silent film actor, (Meridian)
Shauntay Hinton, actress (Starkville)
Eddie Hodges (born 1947), former child actor, (Hattiesburg)

Thelma Houston (born 1943), actress, (Leland)
Don Jeffcoat (born 1975), (Gulfport)
James Earl Jones (born 1931), (Arkabutla)
Robert Earl Jones (1910–2006), (Senatobia)
Simbi Khali (born 1971), (Jackson)
Diane Ladd (born 1935), (Meridian)
Daniel Curtis Lee (born 1991), (Clinton)
Tom Lester (born 1938), (Jackson)
Martha Mattox (1879–1933), silent film actor, (Natchez)
Shane McRae (born 1977), (Starkville)
Gerald McRaney (born 1947), (Collins)
Mary Ann Mobley (born 1939), (Brandon)
Parker Posey (born 1968), (Laurel)
Evelyn Preer (1896–1932), (Vicksburg)
Thalmus Rasulala (1939–1991), (Arkabutla)
Beah Richards (1920–2000), stage/screen/tv actress, (Vicksburg)
Eric Roberts (born 1956), (Biloxi)
Toni Seawright (born 1964), international actress, (Pascagoula)
Larry Semon (1889–1928), silent film actor/director/producer, (West Point)
Jamie Lynn Spears (born 1991), actress and singer, (McComb)
Stella Stevens (born 1938), (Yazoo City)
Tonea Stewart (born 1947), (Greenwood)
Ashley Thompson (born 1980), actress, (Booneville)
James Michael Tyler (born 1962), (Winona)
Brenda Venus (born 1957), actress, (Biloxi)
Ray Walston (1914–2001), (Laurel)
Sela Ward (born 1956), (Meridian)
James Wheaton (1924–2002), (Meridian)
Kit Williamson (born 1985), actor, (Jackson)
Oprah Winfrey (born 1954), (Kosciusko)
Hattie Winston (born 1945), (Greenville)

Artists

Jere Allen, painter, (Oxford)

James McConnell Anderson (1907–1998), potter and painter, (Ocean Springs)

Peter Anderson (1901–1984), potter, (Ocean Springs)

Rick Anderson, painter and children's book illustrator, (Clinton) [5] [6]

Walter Inglis Anderson (1903–1965), painter, (Ocean Springs)

Earl W. Bascom (1906-1995), painter, bronze sculptor, "King of the Cowboy Artists," (Columbia)

Bill Beckwith, sculptor (Taylor) [7] [8]

Howard Bingham (born 1939), photographer, (Jackson)

Jason Bouldin, portrait painter, (Oxford) [9]

Marshall Bouldin III, portrait painter, (Clarksdale) [10]

Bruce Brady, nationally acclaimed sculptor, Sculpted Conerly Trophy, (Brookhaven) [11]

Andrew Bucci (born 1922), painter, (Vicksburg)

Jane Rule Burdine, photographer, (Taylor) [12]

William Dunlap, painter, (Webster County) [13] [14]

Sam Gilliam (born 1933), color field painter, (Tupelo)

Theora Hamblett (1895–1977), painter, (Oxford) [15]

Ted Jackson (born 1955), photographer, (McComb)

Chris LeDoux (1948–2005), bronze sculptor, (Biloxi)

Ed McGowin, sculptor/painter, (Hattiesburg) [16] [17]

Fred Mitchell (born 1923), abstract expressionist painter, (Meridian)

Ethel Wright Mohamed (1906–1992), stitchery artist, (Belzoni) [18] [19]

George E. Ohr (1857–1918), potter, (Biloxi)

J. Kim Sessums, bronze sculptor and painter, (Brookhaven) [20]

Floyd Shaman (died 2005), sculptor, (Cleveland)

Jack Spencer (born 1951), photographer, (Kosciusko)

Glennray Tutor (born 1950), painter, (Oxford)

James W. Washington, Jr. (1908–2000), painter and sculptor, (Gloster)

Dick Waterman (born 1935), photographer and blues promoter, (Oxford)

Athletes and sports-related people
[edit] Baseball

Frank Baker (born 1946), shortstop, (Meridian)
Howard Battle (born 1972), third baseman, (Biloxi)
Cool Papa Bell (1903–1991), center fielder, (Starkville)
Martin Beno (born 1986), pitcher, (Horn Lake)
Don Blasingame (1932–2005), second baseman, (Corinth)
Milt Bolling (born 1930), shortstop, (Mississippi City)
Josh Booty (born 1975), third baseman, (Starkville)
Julio Borbon (born 1986), outfielder, (Starkville)
Dennis Ray "Oil Can" Boyd (born 1959), pitcher, (Meridian)
Jeff Branson (born 1967), infielder, (Waynesboro)
Jeff Brantley (born 1963), pitcher and ESPN analyst, (Starkville)
Adrian Brown (born 1974), center fielder, (McComb)
Jamie Brown (born 1977), pitcher, (Meridian)
Ellis Burks (born 1964), outfielder and designated hitter, (Vicksburg)
Guy Bush (1901–1985), pitcher, (Aberdeen)
Dewon Day (born 1980), relief pitcher, (Jackson)
Dizzy Dean (1910–1974), Hall of Fame pitcher, (Bond)
Tommy Dean (born 1945), shortstop, (Iuka)
Bob Didier (born 1949), catcher, (Hattiesburg)
David "Boo" Ferriss (born 1921), pitcher, (Shaw)
Curt Ford (born 1960), outfielder, (Jackson)
Joey Gathright (born 1981), minor league outfielder, (Hattiesburg)

Jake Gibbs (born 1938), catcher, (Grenada)

Rod Gilbreath (born 1954), second baseman, (Laurel)

Luther Hackman (born 1974), pitcher, (Columbus)

Bill Hall (born 1979), third baseman, (Nettleton)

Mickey Harrington (born 1934), pinch-runner, (Hattiesburg)

Charlie Hayes (born 1965), third baseman, (Hattiesburg)

Larry Herndon (born 1953), outfielder, (Sunflower)

Jarrett Hoffpauir (born 1983), second baseman, (Natchez)

Dusty Hughes (born 1982), relief pitcher (Tupelo)

Cleo James (born 1940), outfielder, (Clarksdale)

Matt Lawton (born 1971), right fielder, (Gulfport)

Brent Leach (born 1982), relief pitcher, (Flowood)

Ronnie Lester (born 1959), player and Assistant General Manager, (Canton)

Fred Lewis (born 1980), left fielder, (Hattiesburg)

John Lindsey (born 1977), minor league first baseman, (Hattiesburg)

Nook Logan (born 1979), center fielder, (Natchez)

Paul Maholm (born 1982), starting pitcher, (Greenwood)

Chris Maloney (born 1961), minor league first baseman/outfielder/manager, (Jackson)

Brian Maxcy (born 1971), pitcher, (Amory)

Allen McDill (born 1971), left-handed specialist pitcher, (Greenville)

Bill Melton (born 1945), third baseman, (Gulfport)

Dustan Mohr (born 1976), outfielder, (Hattiesburg)

Mitch Moreland (born 1985), first baseman & right fielder (Amory)

Ryan Nye (born 1973), pitcher, (Biloxi)

Roy Oswalt (born 1977), starting pitcher, (Weir)

Dave Parker (born 1951), right fielder and designated hitter, (Calhoun)

Claude Passeau (1909–2003), pitcher, (Lucedale)

Van Pope (born 1984), minor league third baseman, (Jackson)

Gary Rath (born 1973), starting pitcher, (Gulfport)
Kevin Rogers (born 1968), pitcher, (Cleveland)
Nate Rolison (born 1977), first baseman, (Petal)
George Scott (born 1944), first baseman, (Greenville)
Tony Sipp (born 1983), relief pitcher, (Moss Point)
Matt Skrmetta (born 1972), pitcher, (Biloxi)
Jason Smith (born 1977), infielder, (Meridian)
Seth Smith (born 1982), outfielder, (Jackson)
Blake Stein (born 1973), pitcher, (McComb)
Craig Tatum (born 1983), catcher (Hattiesburg)
Marcus Thames (born 1977), outfielder and first baseman, (Louisville)
John Thomson (born 1973), starting pitcher, (Vicksburg)
Matt Tolbert (born 1982), infielder, (born in McComb, raised in Woodville)
Eddie "Scooter" Tucker (born 1966), catcher, (Greenville)
Jermaine Van Buren (born 1980), relief pitcher, (Laurel)
Chico Walker (born 1957), second base, (Jackson)
Harry Walker (1916–1999), outfielder and manager, (Pascagoula)
Skeeter Webb (1909–1986), infielder, (Meridian)
Barry Wesson (born 1977), outfielder, (Tupelo)
Frank White (born 1950), second baseman and coach, (Greenville)
Eli Whiteside (born 1979), catcher, (New Albany)
Dmitri Young (born 1973), first baseman, (Vicksburg)
Terrell Young (born 1985), minor league pitcher, (Grenada)
Tim Young (born 1973), relief pitcher, (Gulfport)
Walter Young (born 1980), first baseman, (Hattiesburg)

Basketball

Mahmoud Abdul-Rauf (born 1969), point guard, (Gulfport)
Coolidge Ball, forward, (Indianola)

Earl Barron (born 1981), center, (Clarksdale)
Billy Ray Bates (born 1956), shooting guard, (Kosciusko)
Jonathan Bender (born 1981), power forward, (Picayune)
Travarus Bennett (born 1979), minor leagues, (Rosedale)
Ruthie Bolton (born 1967), shooting guard, head coach (Lucedale)
Melvin Booker (born 1972), point guard, (Pascagoula)
Tom Bowens (born 1940), forward-center, (Okolona)
Alonzo Bradley (born 1953), forward, (Utica)
Rickey Brown (born 1958), forward-center, (Madison County)
Cleveland Buckner (born 1938), forward-center, (Yazoo City)
Jackie Butler (born 1985), center, (McComb)
Maurice Carter (born 1976), guard, (Jackson)
Cornelius Cash (born 1952), forward, (Macon)
Harvey Catchings (born 1951), center, (Jackson)
Terry Catledge (born 1963), forward, (Houston)
Van Chancellor (born 1943), women's coach, (Louisville)
E.C. Coleman (born 1950), forward, (Flora)
Joe Courtney (born 1969), power forward, (Jackson)
Erick Dampier (born 1975), center, (New Hebron)
Ollie Darden (born 1944), forward-center, (Aberdeen)
Archie Dees (born 1936), forward-center, (Ethel)
Ronald Dupree (born 1981), small forward, (Biloxi)
Stephen Dyess (born 1984), small forward, (Meridian) [21] [22]
Keith Edmonson (born 1960), guard, (Gulfport)
Monta Ellis (born 1985), point guard and shooting guard, (Jackson)
Tim Floyd (born 1954), men's head coach, (Hattiesburg)
Nell Fortner (born 1959), women's head coach, (Jackson)
Jennifer Gillom (born 1964), WMBA player/Olympic gold medalist and coach, (Abbeville)
Gerald Glass (born 1967), guard-forward, (Greenwood)
Lancaster Gordon (born 1962), guard-forward, (Jackson)
Litterial Green (born 1970), point guard, (Pascagoula)

Kevin Griffin (born 1975), shooting guard/small forward

Tang Hamilton (born 1978), forward, (Jackson)

Ira Harge (born 1941), center, (Anguilla)

Othella Harrington (born 1974), power forward, (Jackson)

Lusia Harris (born 1955), first female player inducted into the Naismith Memorial Basketball Hall of Fame, (Minter City)

Antonio Harvey (born 1970), radio broadcaster/retired player, (Pascagoula)

Spencer Haywood (born 1949), power forward/center, (Silver City)

Jeanne Ruark Hoff, Stanford University player

Eddie Hughes (born 1960), point guard, (Greenville)

Lindsey Hunter (born 1970), point guard, (Utica)

Leroy Hurd (born 1980), forward, (Pascagoula)

Al Jefferson (born 1985), center/power forward, (Monticello)

Clay Johnson (born 1956), guard, (Yazoo City)

John Johnson (born 1947), small forward, (Carthage)

Trey Johnson (born 1984), shooting guard, (Jackson)

Carolyn Jones-Young (born 1969), guard and Olympic bronze medalist, (Bay Springs)

Randolph Keys (born 1966), guard-forward, (Collins)

Danny Manning (born 1966), forward, (Hattiesburg)

Ed Manning (born 1944), forward, (Summit)

Antonio McDyess (born 1974), power forward, (Quitman)

Derrick McKey (born 1966), small forward and power forward, (Meridian)

Leland Mitchell (born 1941), guard, (Kiln)

Matthew Mitchell (born 1970), women's head coach, (Louisville)

Steve Newsome, Chicago Bulls draft (1973), (Columbia)

Dyron Nix (born 1967), forward, (Meridian)

Audie Norris (born 1960), center, (Jackson)

Willie Norwood (born 1947), forward, (Carrollton)

Travis Outlaw (born 1984), small forward amd power forward, (Starkville)
Murriel Page (born 1975), WNBA player, (Louin)
Marckell Patterson (born 1979), shooting guard, (Eupora)
Kenny Payne (born 1966), small forward, (Laurel)
Armintie Price (born 1985), shooting guard, (Myrtle)
Dolph Pulliam, center, sports broadcaster, (West Point)
Bob Quick (born 1946), guard-forward, (Thornton)
Justin Reed (born 1982), forward, (Jackson)
James Robinson (born 1970), shooting guard, (Jackson)
Eugene Short (born 1953), small forward, (Hattiesburg)
Purvis Short (born 1957), small forward and shooting guard, (Hattiesburg)
Larry Smith (born 1958), center-forward, (Rolling Fork)
Sedric Toney (born 1962), guard, (Columbus)
Jarvis Varnado (born 1988), forward-center
Margaret Wade (1912–1995), former player and coach, (Cleveland)
Cornell Warner (born 1948), forward-center, (Jackson)
Eric Washington (born 1974), guard-forward, (Pearl)
Clarence Weatherspoon (born 1970), power forward, (Crawford)
Dwayne Whitfield (born 1972), power forward, (Aberdeen)
Tamika Whitmore (born 1977), forward, (Tupelo)
Maurice "Mo" Williams (born 1982), point guard, (Jackson)
George Wilson (born 1942), center, (Meridian)

American football

Brian Alford (born 1975), wide receiver, (Crawford)
Jake Allen (born 1985), wide receiver, (Laurel)
Lance Alworth (born 1940), wide receiver, (Brookhaven)
Jesse Anderson (born 1966), tight end, (West Point)
Rashard Anderson (born 1977), cornerback, (Forest)

Houston Antwine (born 1939), defensive tackle, (Louise)

Jason Armstead (born 1979), wide receiver (Canadian Football League), (Moss Point)

Hank Autry (born 1947), center, (Hattiesburg)

Chris Avery (born 1975), fullback and linebacker (arena football), (Grenada)

Jerome Barkum (born 1950), wide receiver/tight end, (Gulfport)

Fred Barnett (born 1966), wide receiver, (Gunnison)

Lem Barney (born 1945), cornerback, (Gulfport)

Steve Baylark (born 1983), running back, (Aberdeen)

Tony Bennett (born 1967), linebacker, (Alligator)

Kenneth Bernich (born 1951), guard, (Biloxi)

Damarius Bilbo (born 1982), football, (Moss Point)

Harold Bishop, Jr. (born 1970), tight end, (Booneville)

Earl Blair (1934–2004), halfback, (Pascagoula)

George Blair (born 1938), AFL halfback, (Pascagoula)

Josh Booty (born 1975), quarterback, (Starkville)

Tim Bowens (born 1973), defensive tackle, (Okolona)

Johnny Brewer (born 1937), tight end/linebacker, (Vicksburg)

Allen Brown (born 1943), tight end, (Natchez)

C. C. Brown (born 1983), safety, (Greenwood)

Nathan Brown (born 1986), quarterback, (Hattiesburg)

Willie Brown (born 1940), cornerback, (Yazoo)

Derrick Burgess (born 1978), defensive end/linebacker, (Oxford)

Chris Burkett (born 1962), wide receiver, (Laurel)

Jason Campbell (born 1981), quarterback, (Laurel)

Steve Campbell (born 1966), head coach

Cooper Carlisle (born 1977), offensive guard, (Greenville)

Alex Carrington (born 1987), defensive lineman, (Tupelo)

Perry Carter (born 1971), defensive back, (McComb)

Kory Chapman (born 1980), running back, (Batesville)

Don Churchwell (born 1936), offensive tackle, (Leakesville)

Billy Clay (born 1944), cornerback, (Oxford)

Roderick (Rod) Coleman (born 1976), defensive tackle, (Vicksburg)

Reggie Collier (born 1961), quarterback and wide receiver, (D'Iberville)

Charlie Conerly (1921–1996), (Clarksdale)

Darion Conner (born 1967), NFL linebacker and Arena Football League player, (Macon)

Fred Cook (born 1952), defensive end, (Pascagoula)

Johnie Cooks (born 1958), linebacker, (Leland)

Russell Copeland (born 1971), wide receiver, (Tupelo)

Bobby Crespino (born 1938), tight end, (Duncan)

Quinton Culberson (born 1985), linebacker, (Jackson

Doug Cunningham (born 1945), running back, (Louisville)

Roland Dale (born 1927), end, (Magee)

Willie Daniel (born 1937), defensive back, (New Albany)

Rod Davis (born 1981), linebacker, (Gulfport)

Mike Dennis (born 1944), running back, (Philadelphia)

Anthony Dixon (born 1987), running back, (Jackson)

Kevin Dockery (born 1984), cornerback, (Hernando)

Larry Dorsey (born 1953), wide receiver and high school coach, (Corinth)

Jim Dunaway (born 1941), defensive tackle, (Columbia)

Marcus Dupree (born 1964), running back, (Philadelphia)

Antuan Edwards (born 1977), safety, (Starkville)

Mario Edwards (born 1975), cornerback, (Gautier)

Carlos Emmons (born 1973), linebacker, (Greenwood)

Mike Espy (born 1982), wide receiver, (Jackson)

Don "Red" Estes[*citation needed*] (born 1938), offensive lineman, (Brookhaven)

Major Everett (born 1960), running back, (New Hebron)

Brett Favre (born 1969), quarterback, (Kiln)

Jason Ferguson (born 1974), defensive tackle, (Nettleton)

Damion Fletcher (born 1987), running back, (Biloxi)

Leslie Frazier (born 1959), cornerback and safety/Defensive Coordinator, (Columbus)

Steve Freeman (born 1953), defensive back, game official, (Oxford)

C. J. Gaddis (born 1985), safety, (Hattiesburg)

William Gaines (born 1971), defensive lineman, (Jackson)

Charles E. Gavin[*citation needed*] (born 1933), defensive end for the Denver Broncos, (Lake)

Jimmie Giles (born 1954), tight end, (Natchez)

Robert Gillespie (born 1979), running back, (Hattiesburg)

Tom Goode (born 1938), offensive lineman, (West Point)

Larry Grantham (born 1938), linebacker, (Crystal Springs)

Hugh Green (born 1959), linebacker, (Natchez)

Louis Green (born 1979), linebacker, (Vicksburg)

L. C. Greenwood (born 1946), defensive end, (Canton)

Jack Gregory (born 1944), defensive end, (Okolona)

Cedric Griffin (born 1982), cornerback, (Natchez)

Glynn Griffing (born 1940), quarterback, (Bentonia)

Justin Griffith (born 1980), fullback, (Magee)

Quentin Groves (born 1984), defensive end, (Greenville)

Michael Haddix (born 1961), running back, (Tippah County)

Bobby Hamilton (born 1971), defensive end, (Columbia)

Parys Haralson (born 1984), linebacker, (Flora)

Larry Hardy (born 1956), tight end, (Mendenhall)

Clarence Harmon (born 1955), running back, (Kosciusko)

Anthony Harris (born 1981), defensive tackle

James Harvey (born 1965), guard, (Columbia)

Kevin Henry (born 1968), defensive lineman, (Mound Bayou)

Mack Herron (born 1948), running back, (Biloxi)

Roy Hilton (born 1943), defensive end, (Hazlehurst)

Stephen Hobbs (born 1965), wide receiver, (Mendenhall)

Corey Holmes (born 1976), running back (Canadian football), (Greenville)

Jaret Holmes (born 1976), placekicker, (Clinton)

Lester Holmes (born 1969), offensive lineman, (Tylertown)
Walter Holman (born 1959), running back, (Vaiden)
Estus Hood (born 1955), cornerback, (Hattiesburg)
Houston Hoover (born 1965), offensive lineman, (Yazoo City)
Joe Horn (born 1972), wide receiver, (Tupelo)
Derrick Hoskins (born 1970), cornerback, (Meridian)
Gary Huff (born 1951), quarterback, (Natchez)
Kent Hull (born 1960), offensive lineman, (Pontotoc)
Don Hultz (born 1940), defensive lineman, (Moss Point)
Terry Irvin (born 1954), defensive back (Canadian Football League), (Columbia)
Brandon Jackson (born 1985), running back, (Horn Lake)
Harold Jackson (born 1946), wide receiver, (Hattiesburg)
Jarious Jackson (born 1977), quarterback/free safety (American and Canadian Football Leagues), (Tupelo)
Kirby Jackson (born 1965), defensive back, (Sturgis)
Tristan Jackson (born 1986), defensive back (Canadian football), (Beaumont)
Sean James (born 1969), running back, (Meridian)
Melvin Jenkins (born 1962), cornerback, (Jackson)
Antonio Johnson (born 1984), defensive tackle, (Greenville)
Dennis Johnson (born 1956), fullback, (Weir)
Rory Johnson (born 1986), linebacker (American and Canadian Football Leagues), (Vicksburg)
Spencer Johnson (born 1981), defensive tackle, (Waynesboro)
Chris Jones (born 1982), wide receiver, (Macon)
Ronald Jones (born 1981), defensive lineman (Canadian Football League), (Gulfport)
Reggie Kelly (born 1977), tight end, (Aberdeen)
Tommy Kelly (born 1980), defensive tackle, (Jackson)
Tyrone Keys (born 1960), defensive lineman, (Jackson)
Ed Khayat (born 1935), defensive end, (Moss Point)
Curt Knight (born 1943), placekicker, (Gulfport)

Roland Lakes (born 1939), defensive lineman/defensive tackle, (Vicksburg)

Donald Lee (born 1980), tight end, (Maben)

Brad Leggett (born 1966), center, (Vicksburg)

Alex Lincoln (born 1977), linebacker, (Meridian)

Ken Lucas (born 1979), cornerback, (Cleveland)

Milton Mack (born 1963), cornerback, (Jackson)

Earsell Mackbee (born 1941), cornerback, (Brookhaven)

John Mangum (born 1967), cornerback, (Magee)

Kris Mangum (born 1973), tight end, (Magee)

Archie Manning (born 1949), quarterback, (Drew)

Eli Manning (born 1981), quarterback, (Oxford)

Mike Markuson (born 1961), offensive line coach and running game coordinator

Aubrey Matthews (born 1962), wide receiver, (Pascagoula)

Shane Matthews (born 1970), quarterback, (Pascagoula)

Fred McAfee (born 1968), running back, (Philadelphia)

Deuce McAllister (born 1978), running back, (Morton)

Trumaine McBride (born 1985), cornerback, (Clarksdale)

Dee McCann (born 1983), cornerback (American and Canadian Football Leagues), (Lucedale)

Dexter McCleon (born 1973), safety, (Meridian)

Sam McCullum (born 1952), wide receiver, (McComb)

Ben McGee (born 1939), defensive end, (Starkville)

Buford McGee (born 1960), running back, (Durant)

Herb McMath (born 1954), defensive tackle and defensive end, (Coahoma)

Greg McMurtry (born 1967), wide receiver, (Jackson)

Fred McNair (born 1968), quarterback, (Mount Olive)

Steve McNair (1973–2009), quarterback, (Mount Olive)

Freeman McNeil (born 1959), running back, (Jackson)

Quinton Meaders (born 1983), defensive back (Canadian Football League), (Tupelo)

Jim Miller (born 1957), punter, (Ripley)

Romaro Miller (born 1978), quarterback, (Shannon)
Freddie Milons (born 1980), wide receiver, (Starkville)
Jayme Mitchell (born 1984), defensive end, (Jackson)
Frank Molden (born 1942), defensive tackle, (Moss Point)
Cleo Montgomery (born 1956), wide receiver, (Greenville)
Wilbert Montgomery (born 1954), running back, (Greenville)
Stevon Moore (born 1967), safety, (Wiggins)
Melvin Morgan (born 1953), defensive back, (Gulfport)
Eric Moulds (born 1973), wide receiver, (Lucedale)
Michael Myers (born 1976), defensive tackle, (Vicksburg)
John Nix (born 1976), defensive lineman (arena football), (Lucedale)
Jerious Norwood (born 1983), running back, (Jackson)
Freddie Joe Nunn (born 1962), defensive end/linebacker, (Noxubee County)
Michael Oher (born 1986), offensive tackle, (Oxford)
Will Overstreet (born 1979), linebacker, (Jackson)
Joe Owens (born 1946), defensive end, (Columbia)
Eddie Payton (born 1951), running back, (Columbia)
Walter Payton (1954–1999), half back, (Columbia)
Derek Pegues (born 1986), safety, (Batesville)
Marlo Perry (born 1972), linebacker, (Forest)
Vernon Perry (born 1953), cornerback, (Jackson)
Stephen Peterman (born 1982), offensive guard, (Gulfport)
Danny Pierce (born 1948), running back, (Laurel)
Lawrence Pillers (born 1952), defensive end, (Hazelhurst)
Todd Pinkston (born 1977), wide receiver, (Forest)
Clinton Portis (born 1981), running back, (Laurel)
Jeff Posey (born 1975), linebacker, (Bassfield)
Clyde Powers (born 1951), safety, (Pascagoula)
Glover Quin (born 1986), cornerback, (McComb)
Eddie Ray (born 1947), running back, (Vicksburg)
Oscar Reed (born 1944), running back, (Jonestown)
Johnny Rembert (born 1961), linebacker, (Hollandale)

Will Renfro (born 1932), offensive tackle, (Batesville)
Jerry Rice (born 1962), wide receiver, (Starkville)
Bobby Richards (born 1938), defensive linemen, (Columbus)
Gloster Richardson (born 1942), wide receiver, (Greenville)
Willie Richardson (born 1939), wide receiver, (Clarksdale)
Dwayne Rudd (born 1976), linebacker, (Batesville)
Tyrone Rush (born 1971), running back, (Meridian)
Jamarca Sanford (born 1985), safety, (Batesville)
John Sawyer (born 1953), tight end, (Brookhaven)
Cedric Scott (born 1977), defensive tackle (Canadian Football League), (Gulfport)
Billy Shaw (born 1938), offensive guard, (Natchez)
Harold Shaw (born 1974), fullback and occasional linebacker, (Magee)
Billy Shields (born 1953), tackle, (Vicksburg)
Kendall Simmons (born 1979), guard, (Ripley)
Terrance Simmons (born 1976), defensive tackle, (Moss Point)
Jackie Slater (born 1954), offensive tackle, (Jackson)
Jackie Smith (born 1940), tight end, (Columbia)
Jimmy Smith (born 1969), wide receiver, (Jackson)
Noland Smith (born 1943), wide receiver/return specialist, (Jackson)
Armegis Spearman (born 1978), linebacker, (Oxford)
Chris Spencer (born 1982), center, (Madison)
Irving Spikes (born 1970), running back, (Ocean Springs)
Billy Stacy (born 1936), safety, (Drew)
Thomas Strauthers (born 1961), defensive lineman, (Wesson)
Diron Talbert (born 1944), defensive tackle, (Pascagoula)
Don Talbert (born 1939), offensive tackle, (Louisville)
Daryl Terrell (born 1975), offensive lineman, (Vossburg)
Fred Thomas (born 1973), cornerback, (Bruce)
Norris Thomas (born 1954), cornerback, (Inverness)
Eric Tillman (born c.1957), general manager of the Canadian Football League, (Jackson)

Lewis Tillman (born 1966), running back, (Hazlehurst)
Billy Tohill (born c.1939), head coach, (Batesville)
Willie Totten (born 1962), head coach, (Leflore County)
Deshea Townsend (born 1975), cornerback, (Batesville)
Bill Triplett (born 1940), running back, (Shaw)
Billy Truax (born 1943), tight end, (Gulfport)
Jim Urbanek (born 1945), defensive tackle, (Oxford)
Gerald Vaughn (born 1970), defensive back (Canadian Football League), (Abbeville)
Jim Walden (born c.1938), head coach, (Aberdeen)
Kenyatta Walker (born 1979), offensive tackle, (Meridian)
Gavin Walls (born 1980), defensive end (Canadian Football League), (Ripley)
Wesley Walls (born 1966), tight end, (Batesville)
Tom Walters (born 1942), safety, (Petal)
Swayze Waters (born 1987), kicker, (Jackson)
Kendell Watkins (born 1973), tight end, (Jackson)
Willie West (born 1938), defensive back, (Lexington)
Chris White (born 1983), guard, (Winona)
Larry Whigham (born 1972), cornerback, (Hattiesburg)
Ben Williams (born 1954), defensive lineman, (Yazoo City)
Grant Williams (born 1974), offensive tackle, (Hattiesburg)
Greg Williams (born 1959), safety, (Greenville)
John Williams (born 1947), offensive lineman, (Jackson)
Sammy Williams (born 1974), offensive tackle, (Magnolia)
Odell Willis (born 1984), defensive lineman (American and Canadian Football Leagues), (Meridian)
Sammy Winder (born 1959), running back, (Madison)
Mike Withycombe (born 1964), guard, (Meridian)
Otis Wonsley (born 1957), running back, (Pascagoula)
Lee Woodruff (1909–unknown), running back, (Batesville)
Keith Woodside (born 1964), running back, (Natchez)
Abe Woodson (born 1934), cornerback/kick returner, (Jackson)

Marv Woodson (born 1941), defensive back, (Hattiesburg)

Floyd Womack (born 1978), offensive tackle, (Cleveland)

Cornelius Wortham (born 1982), linebacker, (Calhoun City)

Other sports

Fletcher Abram (born 1950), Olympic handball player, (Cary)

Trey Alexander (born 1983), professional soccer midfielder, (Meridian)

Earl W. Bascom (1906-1995), rodeo, Hall of Fame, "Father of Mississippi Rodeo," (Columbia)

Ralph Boston (born 1939), Olympic long jumper, (Laurel)

Devin Britton (born 1991), tennis player, (Jackson)

Lee Calhoun (1933–1989), Olympic track athlete and college track coach, (Laurel)

Shelby Cannon (born 1966), professional tennis player, (Hattiesburg)

Floyd Cummings (born 1949), heavyweight boxer

Tony Dees (born 1963), Olympic hurdler, (Pascagoula)

Craig Demmin (born 1971), soccer defender

Ted DiBiase (born 1954), professional wrestler, (Clinton)

Ted DiBiase Jr (born 1982), professional wrestler, (Clinton)

Barbara Ferrell (born 1947), Olympic track athlete, (Hattiesburg)

Jim Gallagher, Jr. (born 1961), professional golfer, (Greenwood)

Bobby Hamilton (1957–2007), NASCAR driver, (Columbia)

Otis Harris (born 1982), Olympic track and field athlete, (Edwards)

Jimmy Hart (born 1944), professional wrestling manager, (Jackson)

Josh Hayes (born 1975), professional motorcycle roadracer, (Gulfport)

Floyd Heard (born 1966), track and field sprinter, (West Point)

Leroy Jones (born 1950), professional boxer, (Meridian)

Justin Mapp (born 1984), professional soccer player, (Brandon)
Kennedy McKinney (born 1966), professional boxer, (Hernando)
Coby Miller (born 1976), track and field athlete, (Ackerman)
Mary Mills (born 1940), professional golfer, (Laurel)
Larry Myricks (born 1956), Olympic long jumper, (Clinton)
Terri O'Connell, motorsports racer, (Corinth)
Reed Pierce (born 1963), professional pool player, (Jackson)
Brittney Reese (born 1986), Olympic long jumper, (Gulfport)
Kevin Robertson (born 1959), Olympic water polo player, (Biloxi)
Chris Shivers (born 1978), professional bull rider, (Natchez)
Calvin Smith (born 1961), Olympic sprinter, (Bolton)
Lake Speed (born 1948), NASCAR driver, (Jackson)
Ricky Stenhouse, Jr. (born 1987), stock car driver, (Olive Branch)
Dallas Stewart (born 1959), thoroughbred horse trainer, (McComb)
Ernie Terrell (born 1939), former WBA heavyweight boxing champion, (Belzoni)
Charles Walker (born 1934), checkers champion and minister, (Petal)
Herb Washington (born 1951), sprinter/pinch runner, (Belzoni)

Broadcast media personalities

Red Barber (1908–1992), sportscaster, (Columbus)
Alex Bonner (1926–2003), broadcast media executive, (Marks)
Campbell Brown (born 1968), CNN anchor, (Natchez)
Ron Franklin (born 1942), ESPN sportscaster, (Jackson)
Paul Gallo (born 1947), radio host, (Shaw)
Chris McDaniel (born 1971), talk radio host, (Laurel)
Angela McGlowan, Fox News political commentator, (Oxford)

Robin Roberts (born 1960), newscaster, (Pass Christian)
Norman Robinson (born 1951), news anchor, (Toomsuba)
Doug Russell (born 1972), sportscaster, (Jackson)
Tavis Smiley (born 1964), talk show host, (Gulfport)
Shepard Smith (born 1964), Fox News anchor, (Holly Springs)
Bob Sullender, (born 1973), sportscaster, (Clinton)
Oprah Winfrey (born 1954), talk show host, (Kosciusko)

Comedians

Jerry Clower (1926–1998), (Liberty)
David L. Cook (born 1968), (Pascagoula)
Mack Dryden (born 1949), (Moss Point)
Tig Notaro, stand-up comedy, (Jackson)

Educators

James Madison Carpenter (1888–1983), folklorist, (Prentiss County)

Jesse Dukeminier (1925–2003), professor of law, (West Point)

William R. Ferris (born 1942), folklorist, chairman of National Endowment for the Humanities, (Vicksburg)

George W. Grace (born 1921), linguist, (Corinth)

Robert Khayat (born 1938), chancellor of the University of Mississippi, (Moss Point)

Mamie Locke (born 1954), political scientist, dean at Hampton University, (Brandon)

John A. Lomax (1867-1948), folklorist, (Goodman)

Frances Lucas (born 1957), president of Millsaps College, (Jackson)

Walter E. Massey (born 1938), physicist, University of Chicago, (Hattiesburg)

William H. Miller (born 1941), theoretical chemist, (Kosciusko)

William Muse, chancellor at East Carolina University

Rod Paige (born 1933), U.S. secretary of education, (Monticello)

Roy Vernon Scott (born 1927), historian, (Starkville)

Jimmy G. Shoalmire (1940-1982), historian (Starkville)

Louis Westerfield (born 1949), law professor, first African-American Dean of the University of Mississippi School of Law, (De Kalb)

Fannie C. Williams (1882–1980), normal school educator (Biloxi)

Entrepreneurs/Business leaders

Jim Barksdale (born 1943), president and CEO of Netscape, (Jackson)

James Breckenridge Speed (1844–1912), industrial pioneer

Fred Carl, Jr., founder of Viking Range Corporation, (Greenwood)

Cully Cobb (1884-1975), agricultural publisher

Bernard "Bernie" Ebbers (born 1941), founder and CEO of WorldCom, convicted of fraud and conspiracy, (Brookhaven)

Joshua Green (1869–1975), shipping magnate, banker, (Jackson)

Sam Haskell (born 1955), former worldwide head of television for the William Morris Agency, (Amory)[23]

Robert L. Johnson (born 1946), founder of Black Entertainment Television, (Hickory)

Ken Lewis (born 1947), Chairman, CEO, and President of Bank of America Corporation, (Meridian)

Walter E. Massey (born 1938), corporate executive and board member of several oganizations, (Hattiesburg)

Glenn McCullough (born 1954), chairman and CEO of GLM Associates, LLC, (Tupelo)

Charles Moorman (born 1953), CEO of Norfolk Southern, (Hattiesburg)

Clarence Otis, Jr. (born 1956), CEO of Darden Restaurants, (Vicksburg)

Hartley Peavey (born 1941), founder of Peavey Electronics, (Starkville)

Pig Foot Mary (1870–1929), culinary entrepreneur, (Mississippi Delta)

Robert "Bob" Pittman, founder MTV, former CEO and COO AOL, (Jackson)

J. H. Rush (1868–1931), founder of Rush's Infirmary, the first private hospital in Meridian, Mississippi, (De Kalb)

Fred Smith (born 1944), founder of FedEx, (Marks)

Antonio Maceo Walker (1909–1994), president of the Universal Life Insurance Company of Memphis, Tennessee, (Indianola)

[edit] Filmmakers

Charles Burnett (born 1944), (Vicksburg)

Jamaa Fanaka (born 1942), (Jackson)

John Fortenberry, film and television director, (Jackson)

Lawrence Gordon (born 1936), producer of Die Hard and other films, (Yazoo City)

Jonathan Murray (born 1955), creator of the reality TV genre, (Gulfport)

Patrik-Ian Polk (born 1973), (Hattiesburg)

Larry A. Thompson (born 1944), television and film producer, (Clarksdale)

Inventors

Earl W. Bascom (1906-1995), inventor of rodeo equipment, (Columbia)

Harry A. Cole, inventor of Pine-Sol, (Jackson)

Joseph Newman, inventor of the Newman motor, (Lucedale)

Henry Sampson (born 1934), inventor, (Jackson)

Jurists and lawyers

Rhesa H. Barksdale (born 1944), federal judge (Jackson)

Neal Brooks Biggers Jr. (born 1935), federal judge (Corinth)

William Joel Blass (born 1917), attorney, (Wiggins/Gulfport)

Gerald Chatham (1906–1956), lawyer, lead prosecutor in the Emmett Till case, (Hernando)

Bobby DeLaughter (born 1954), prosecutor, judge (Jackson)

Jess H. Dickinson (born 1947), associate justice, Supreme Court of Mississippi, (Charleston)

Boyce Holleman (1924-2003), attorney, (Wiggins/Gulfport)

Frank Hunger (born 1936), assistant U.S. attorney general, (Greenville)[24]

E. Grady Jolly (born 1937), judge of the U.S. Fifth Circuit Court of Appeals, (Louisville)

Charles W. Pickering (born 1937), federal judge, (Jones County)

Thomas Rodney (1744–1811), federal judge, (Natchez)

Richard "Dickie" Scruggs (born 1946), attorney, (Pascagoula)

Michael B. Thornton (born 1954), judge, U.S. Tax Court

Michael Wallace (born 1951), lawyer, (Biloxi)

James R. Williams (born 1936), lawyer and jurist, (Columbus)

Military figures

William Wirt Adams (1819–1888), brigadier general, CSA, (Jackson)

Van T. Barfoot (born 1919), World War II colonel and Medal of Honor recipient, (Edinburg)

William Barksdale (1821–1863), brigadier general, CSA, died at Gettysburg, (Jackson)

William Billingsley (1887–1913), ensign, first Navy aviator killed in an airplane crash, (Winona)

Alvin C. Cockrell (1918–1942), second lieutenant, USMC, killed in World War II, (Hazelhurst)

Nathan Bedford Forrest (1821–1877), general, CSA, (Hernando)

Walter "Smokey" Gordon (1920-1997), World War II veteran, portrayed in the HBO mini-series Band Of Brothers[citation needed]

Jeffery Hammond (born 1978), major general, (Hattiesburg)

Randolph M. Holder (1918–1942), USN lieutenant (junior grade), (Jackson)

Felix Huston (1800–1857), general, Texas army, (Natchez)

Samuel Reeves Keesler (1896–1918), airman, WWI, (Greenwood)

Newton Knight (1837–1922), Unionist guerrilla leader, (Jones County)

Roy Joseph Marchand (1920–1942), World War II fireman first class, (Crandall)

Henry Pinckney McCain (1861–1941), adjutant general, US Army, (Carroll County)

John S. McCain, Sr. (1884–1945), USN admiral, (Teoc)

Donald H. Peterson (born 1933), USAF colonel and NASA astronaut, (Winona)

Charles Read (1840–1890), naval officer, (Meridian)

Viola B. Sanders (born 1921), USN captain, director of women, U.S. Navy, (Sidon)

Daniel Isom Sultan (1885–1947), inspector general, U.S. Army, (Oxford)

James Monroe Trotter (1842–1892), first man of color to achieve rank of 2nd Lieutenant, U.S. Army, music historian, (Gulfport)

Richard H. Truly (born 1937), retired United States Navy, former astronaut, and NASA administrator, (Fayette)

[edit] Models

Jennifer Adcock (born 1980), Miss Mississippi 2002 and Miss Mississippi USA 2005, (Hattiesburg)

Kristi Addis (born 1971), Miss Teen USA 1987, (Holcomb)

Susan Akin (born 1965), Miss Mississippi 1985 and Miss America 1986, (Meridian)

Jenna Edwards (born 1981), former Miss Florida and Miss Florida USA, (Brandon)

Ruth Ford (born 1915), model, (Hazlehurst)

Taryn Foshee, Miss Mississippi 2006, (Clinton)

June Juanico (born 1938), beauty queen known for dating Elvis Presley in 1955 and 1956, (Biloxi)

Nan Kelley, Miss Mississippi 1985 and GAC's Top 20 Country Countdown hostess, (Hattiesburg)

Kendra King, Miss Mississippi USA 2006, (Monticello)

Christine Kozlowski, Miss Mississippi 2008, (D'Iberville)

Leah Laviano (born 1988), Miss Mississippi USA 2008, and 1st runner up in Miss USA 2008, (Ellisville)

Monica Louwerens (born 1973), Miss Mississippi 1995, (Greenville)

Lypsinka (born 1955), drag performer and model, (Hazlehurst)

Lynda Lee Mead (born c.1939), Miss America 1960, (Natchez)

Mary Ann Mobley (born 1939), Miss America 1959, (Brandon)

Kimberly Morgan (born 1983), Miss Mississippi 2007, (Taylor)

Cheryl Prewitt (born 1957), Miss America 1980, (Ackerman)

Toni Seawright (born 1964), Miss Mississippi 1987 (first African-American winner), (Pascagoula)

Naomi Sims (1948–2009), fashion model and author (Oxford)

Ellen Stratton (born 1939), model and Playboy Playmate, (Marietta)

Amy Wesson (born 1977), fashion model, (Tupelo)

Cindy Williams (born 1964), journalist and Miss Mississippi USA 1986

Jalin Wood (born 1981), Miss Mississippi 2004 and Miss Mississippi USA 2007, (Waynesboro)

Musicians and performers

3 Doors Down, band, (Escatawpa)

John Luther Adams (born 1953), composer of music inspired by nature, (Meridian)

Afroman (born 1974), comedy rapper, (Hattiesburg)

Tommy Aldridge (born 1950), drummer for Ozzy Osbourne and Whitesnake, (Pearl)

Mose Allison (born 1927), jazz musician, (Tallahatchie County)

Robert Anderson (1919–1995), gospel singer-composer and pianist, (Anguilla)

Steve Azar (born 1964), country singer, (Greenville)

Glen Ballard (born 1953), songwriter and record producer, (Natchez)

David Banner (born 1973), rapper/producer, (Jackson)

Matt Barlow (born 1970), lead singer of the metal band Iced Earth, (Biloxi)

Prentiss Barnes (1925–2006), rhythm and blues singer, (Magnolia)

Lance Bass (born 1979), member of pop group 'N Sync, (Laurel)

Jeff Bates (born 1963), country music singer-songwriter, (Bunker Hill)

Beanland, jam band, (Oxford)

Robert Belfour (born 1940), blues musician, (Holly Springs)

Carey Bell (1936–2007), Chicago blues harmonica player, (Macon)

Big Time Sarah (born 1953), blues singer, (Coldwater)

The Blackwood Brothers, gospel singers, (Choctaw County)

James Blackwood (1919–2002), one of The Blackwood Brothers, (Choctaw County)

Blind Melon, Alternative rock and jam band, (Starkville)

Blind Mississippi Morris (born 1955), blues artist, (Clarksdale)

Blue Mountain, alternative country band, (Oxford)

Lucille Bogan (1897–1948), blues singer, (Amory)

Charley Booker (1925–1989), blues singer and guitarist, (Moorhead)

Eddie Boyd (1914–1994), blues musician, (Clarksdale)

Bobby Bradford (born 1934), jazz musician and composer, (Cleveland)

Jan Bradley (born 1943), soul singer, (Byhalia)

Cory Branan (born 1975), singer-songwriter, (Southhaven)

Jackie Brenston (1930–1979), American R&B singer and saxophonist, (Clarksdale)

Big Bill Broonzy (1898–1958), blues singer-songwriter and guitarist, (Scott County)

Eddie "Bongo" Brown (1932–1984), percussionist, (Clarksdale)

Jimmy Buffett (born 1946), multi-genre singer-songwriter, (Pascagoula)

R. L. Burnside (1926–2005), blues singer-songwriter, (Harmontown)

Jerry Butler (born 1939), soul singer-songwriter, (Sunflower)

Cadillac Don & J-Money, rap duo, (Crawford)

G. C. Cameron (born 1945), soul and R&B singer, (Jackson)

Ace Cannon (born 1934), tenor and alto saxophonist, (Grenada)

Gus Cannon (1883–1979), jug band musician, (Red Banks)

Bo Carter (1893–1964), blues singer, (Bolton)

Johnny Carver (born 1940), country singer, (Jackson)

The Chambers Brothers, soul music group, (Lee County)

Sam Chatmon (1897–1983), blues singer, brother of Bo Carter, (Bolton)

Otis Clay (born 1942), R&B and soul musician, (Waxhaw)

Chalmers Clifton (1889–1966), conductor and composer, (Jackson)

Odia Coates (1942–1991), singer, (Vicksburg)

Hank Cochran (born 1935), country music singer-songwriter, (Isola)

Bill Coday (1942–2008), singer, (Coldwater)

Phil Cohran (born 1927), jazz musician, (Oxford)

Colour Revolt, indie rock band, (Oxford)

Mike Compton (born 1956), bluegrass mandolin player, (Meridian)

David L. Cook (born 1968), Christian country music singer-songwriter, (Pascagoula)

Sam Cooke (1931–1964), (Clarksdale)

The Cook Family Singers, Christian country music group, (Pascagoula)

The Cooters, punk metal band, (Oxford)

James Cotton (born 1935), blues harmonica player and singer-songwriter, (Tunica)

Arthur "Big Boy" Crudup (1905–1974), Delta blues singer and guitarist, (Forest)

Olu Dara (born 1941), jazz musician, (Natchez)

Lester Davenport (1932–2009), American blues harmonica player and singer, (Tchula)

Paul Davis (1948–2008), singer-songwriter, (Meridian)

Jimmy Dawkins (born 1936), blues guitarist and singer, (Tchula)

Al Denson (born 1960), contemporary Christian artist, (Starkville)

Bo Diddley (1928–2008), rock & roll/R&B singer-songwriter, (McComb)

Willie Dixon (1915–1992), blues bassist/singer-ongwriter/record producer, (Vicksburg)

Nate Dogg (born 1969), West Coast Hip Hop and R&B artist, (Clarksdale)

Marshall Drew (born 1984), folk rock singer-songwriter, (Clarksdale)

Kevin Dukes (born 1956), guitarist, (Brookhaven)

Omar Kent Dykes (born 1950), blues guitarist and singer, (McComb)

Judy Dunaway (born 1964), avant-garde composer/free improvisor/conceptual sound artist

Meredith Edwards (born 1984), country singer, (Clinton)

Lehman Engel (1910–1982), composer and conductor, (Jackson)

Shelly Fairchild (born 1977), country music artist, (Clinton)

Charlie Feathers (1932–1998), (Holly Springs)

Five Blind Boys of Mississippi, gospel singers, (Piney Woods)

Steve Forbert (born 1955), pop music singer-songwriter, (Meridian)

Barbara Siggers Franklin (1917–1952), gospel singer and mother of Aretha Franklin, (Shelby)

Lee Garrett, R&B singer-songwriter

Eric "Red Mouth" Gebhardt, multi-genre singer-songwriter, (Biloxi)

Bobbie Gentry (born 1944), singer-songwriter, (Greenwood)

Mickey Gilley (born 1936), country singer and musician, (Natchez)

Mark Gray (born 1952), country music singer and keyboardist, (Vicksburg)

Garland Green (born 1942), soul singer and pianist, (Dunleith)

Lloyd Green (born 1937), country music steel guitarist, (Leaf)

Ted Hawkins (born 1936), singer and songwriter, (Biloxi)

Kenneth Haxton (1919–2002), composer, (Greenville)[25]

Jessie Mae Hemphill (1923–2006), blues musician, (Como)

Caroline Herring, bluegrass musician, (Canton) Michael Henderson (born 1951), bass guitarist, R&B singer (Yazoo City)

Faith Hill (born 1967), country/pop singer, (Jackson)

Kim Hill (born 1963), Christian singer-songwriter, (Starkville)

Ernie Hines (born 1938), soul musician Milt Hinton (1910–2000), jazz double bassist, (Vicksburg)

John Lee Hooker (1917–2001), singer-songwriter and blues guitarist, (Clarksdale)

Big Walter Horton (1917–1981), blues harmonica player, (Horn Lake)

Son House (1902–1988), blues singer and guitarist, (Riverton)

Randy Houser (born 1975), country music artist, (Lake)

Thelma Houston (born 1943), R&B singer-songwriter, (Leland)

Guy Hovis (born 1941), big band singer, (Tupelo)

Howlin' Wolf (1910–1976), blues singer/guitarist/harmonica player, (West Point)

Cary Hudson, lead singer and guitarist for alternative country band Blue Mountain, (Sumrall)

Mississippi John Hurt (c.1893–1966), country blues singer and guitarist, (Teoc)

Clifton Hyde (born 1976), multi-instrumentalist and producer, (Hattiesburg)

Carl Jackson (born 1953), country and bluegrass musician, (Louisville)

Elmore James (1918–1963), blues guitarist and singer-songwriter, (Richland)

Skip James (1902–1969), Delta blues guitarist/pianist/singer-songwriter, (Bentonia)

Roosevelt Jamison (born 1936), songwriter/publicist, (Olive Branch)

Jai Johanny "Jaimoe" Johanson (born 1944), drummer in The Allman Brothers Band, (Ocean Springs)

Big Jack Johnson (born 1940), blues musician, (Clarksdale)

Jimmy Johnson (born 1928), blues guitarist and singer, (Holly Springs)

Robert Johnson (1911–1938), blues and Delta blues musician, (Hazlehurst)

Syl Johnson (born 1936), blues and soul singer, (Holly Springs)

Margie Joseph (born 1950), R&B and soul singer, (Pascagoula)

Junior Kimbrough (1930–1998), blues artist, (Hudsonville)

Albert King (1923–1992), blues guitarist and singer, (Indianola)

B. B. King (born 1925), blues guitarist and singer-songwriter, (Itta Bena)

Fern Kinney, rhythm & blues and disco music entertainer, (Jackson)

Fred Knoblock (born 1953), country singer-songwriter, (Jackson)

Kudzu Kings, band, (Oxford)

Sonny Landreth (born 1951), blues musician and slide guitar player, (Canton)

Denise LaSalle (born 1939), urban contemporary and contemporary R&B singer-songwriter/record producer, (Belzoni)

Rick Lawson (born 1973), soul and R&B singer, (Raymond)

Chris LeDoux (1948–2005), country music singer-songwriter, (Biloxi)

Mylon LeFevre (born 1944), gospel and Christian rock singer, (Gulfport)

J. B. Lenoir (1929–1967), guitarist and singer-songwriter, (Monticello)

Robert "Squirrel" Lester (born 1942), second tenor of The Chi-Lites, (McComb)

Bobby Lounge (born 1950), singer-songwriter, (McComb)

Tommy McClennan (1908–c.1962), Delta blues singer and guitarist, (Yazoo City)

George McConnell, guitarist, (Vicksburg)

Kansas Joe McCoy (1905–1950), blues musician and songwriter, (Raymond)

Papa Charlie McCoy (1909–1950), Delta blues musician and songwriter, (Jackson)

Fred McDowell (1904–1972), blues singer and guitarist, (Como)

Mulgrew Miller (born 1955), jazz pianist, (Greenwood)

Little Milton (1934–2005), blues and soul vocalist and guitarist, (Inverness)

Hoyt Ming, old-time fiddler, (Choctaw County)[26]

Mississippi Mass Choir, gospel choir, (Jackson)

Mississippi Slim (born 1923), country singer and guitarist, (Smithville)

Monkey Joe, blues musician, (Jackson)

Dorothy Moore (born 1947), pop/R&B/gospel singer, (Jackson)

Johnny B. Moore (born 1950), blues singer and guitarist, (Clarksdale)

Charlie Musselwhite (born 1944), blues-harp player and bandleader, (Kosciusko)

Bill Myrick (born 1926), country singer/musician/writer/producer/disc jockey, (Simpson County)

North Mississippi Allstars, blues-rock/jam band, (Hernando)

Brandy Norwood (born 1979), R&B singer-songwriter/record producer, (McComb)

Willie Norwood (born 1955), gospel singer, (McComb)

Alexander O'Neal (born 1953), soul singer, (Natchez)

Paul Overstreet (born 1955), country music singer-songwriter, (Newton)

Ginny Owens, blind contemporary Christian music singer-songwriter, (Jackson)

Junior Parker (1932–1971), Memphis blues singer and musician, (Clarksdale)

Michael Passons (born 1965), founding member of the Christian band Avalon, (Yazoo City)

Charley Patton (1891–1934), Delta-/Country-/Gospel blues musician, (Edwards)

Dion Payton (born 1950), blues guitarist and singer, (Greenwood)

Elvis Presley (1935–1977), multi-genre musician, (Tupelo)

Leontyne Price (born 1927), opera singer, (Laurel)

Charley Pride (born 1938), country music singer, (Sledge)

John Primer (born 1945), blues singer and guitarist, (Camden)

Stephen Purdy (born 1970), conductor/pianist and vocal coach for broadway musicals and broadway actors, (Hattiesburg)

Ray J (born 1981), contemporary R&B and hip hop singer/record producer, (McComb)

Jimmy Reed (1925–1976), blues singer and musician, (Dunleith)

Del Rendon (1965–2005), country musician, (Starkville)

Mack Rice (born 1933), songwriter, (Clarksdale)

LeAnn Rimes (born 1982), country and pop singer, (Pearl)

Fenton Robinson (born 1935), blues musician, (Greenwood)

Jimmie Rodgers (1897–1933), country singer, (Meridian)

Jimmy Rogers (1924–1997), blues singer and guitarist, (Ruleville)

David Ruffin (1941–1991), former lead singer of The Temptations, (Whynot)

Jimmy Ruffin (born 1939), soul and R&B singer, (Collinsville)

Bobby Rush (born 1940), blues and R&B musician/composer/singer, (Jackson)

Otis Rush (born 1935), blues musician, (Philadelphia)

Oliver Sain (1932–2003), saxophonist/drummer/songwriter/record producer, (Dundee)

Magic Sam (1937–1969), Chicago blues and soul blues musician, (Grenada) Jeff Savage, Grammy/Dove winning pop producer and songwriter/film composer, (Clinton)[citation needed] Scott Savage, drummer for Christian rock band Jars of Clay, (Clinton) Saving Abel, rock band, (Corinth)

Johnny Sea (born 1940), country singer, (Gulfport)

Toni Seawright (born 1964), singer-songwriter, (Pascagoula)

Jumpin' Gene Simmons (1933–2006), rockabilly singer, (Tupelo)

Byther Smith (born 1933), blues musician, (Monticello)

Soulja Boy (born 1990), rapper/record producer, (Batesville)

Otis Spann (1930–1970), blues musician, (Jackson)

Britney Spears (born 1981), pop singer, (McComb)

Judson Spence (born 1965), songwriter and multi-instrumentalist, (Pascagoula)

Roebuck "Pop" Staples (1914–2000), founder of The Staple Singers, (Winona)

Rogers Stevens (born 1970), guitarist for the band Blind Melon, (West Point)

Lisa Stewart (born 1968), country musician, (Louisville)

William Grant Still (1895–1978), classical composer, (Woodville)

Barrett Strong (born 1941), singer and songwriter, (West Point)

Marty Stuart (born 1958), country music singer, (Philadelphia)

Hubert Sumlin (born 1931), blues musician, (Greenwood)

Deanna Summers, songwriter Ty Tabor (born 1961), guitarist/songwriter/vocalist for rock band King's X, (Pearl)

Eddie Taylor (1923–1985), blues guitarist and singer, (Benoit)

Hound Dog Taylor (1915–1975), blues guitarist and singer, (Natchez)

Melvin Taylor (born 1959), blues musician, (Jackson) Ernie Terrell (born 1939), singer and record producer, (Belzoni)

Jean Terrell (born 1944), R&B and jazz singer, (Belzoni)

James "Son" Thomas (1926–1993), blues musician, (Leland)

Rufus Thomas (1917–2001), R&B/funk/soul singer, (Cayce)

Ashley Thompson (born 1980), singer, (Booneville)

Ike Turner (1931–2007), multi-genre musician/record producer, (Clarksdale)

Conway Twitty (1933–1993), country singer-songwriter, (Friars Point)

Freddie Waits (1943–1989), hard bop and post-bop drummer, (Jackson)

Travis Wammack (born 1944), rock and roll guitarist, (Walnut)

Walter Ward (born 1940), R&B singer and lead vocalist of The Olympics, (Jackson)

Muddy Waters (1913–1983), Electric blues and Chicago blues musician, (Rolling Fork)

Jim Weatherly (born 1943), country and pop singer-songwriter, (Pontotoc)

Carl Weathersby (born 1953), blues vocalist/guitarist/songwriter, (Jackson)

Boogie Bill Webb (1924-1990), blues guitarist and singer, (Jackson)

Bukka White (1909–1977), Delta blues guitarist and singer, (Houston)

Carson Whitsett (1945–2007), keyboardist and songwriter, (Jackson)

Tim Whitsett (born 1943), band leader/songwriter/producer, (Jackson)

Webb Wilder (born 1954), country/surf music/rock & roll musician, (Hattiesburg)

Big Joe Williams (1903–1982), Delta blues musician and songwriter, (Crawford)

Hayley Williams (born 1988), pop punk and alternative rock singer-songwriter, (Meridian)

Sonny Boy Williamson II (died 1965), blues harmonica player and singer-songwriter, (Glendora)

Eddie Willis (born 1936), electric guitarist, (Grenada)

Al Wilson (1939–2008), singer and drummer, (Meridian)

Cassandra Wilson (born 1955), jazz singer-songwriter, (Jackson)

Mary Wilson (born 1944), singer and founding member of The Supremes, (Greenville) Elder Roma Wilson (born 1910), harmonica player, (Blue Springs)[*citation needed*]

Tammy Wynette (1942–1998), country music singer-songwriter, (Tremont)

Lester Young (1909–1959), jazz tenor saxophonist and clarinetist, (Woodville)

Zora Young (born 1948), blues singer, (West Point)

Physicians

Blair E. Batson, chairman of pediatrics at the University of Mississippi Medical Center and namesake of the Blair E. Batson Hospital for Children, (Jackson)

Henry Cloud (born 1956), clinical psychologist, (Vicksburg)

Arthur Guyton (1919–2003), wrote the *Textbook of Medical Physiology*, (Oxford)

John Hall, continues to work on Textbook of Medical Physiology[27]

James Hardy (1918–2003), surgeon who performed the first successful cadaveric lung transplant, (Jackson)[28]

T. R. M. Howard (1908–1976), surgeon and activist, (Mound Bayou)

Thomas Naum James (born 1925), cardiologist, (Amory)

Physicians

Blair E. Batson, chairman of pediatrics at the University of Mississippi Medical Center and namesake of the Blair E. Batson Hospital for Children, (Jackson)

Henry Cloud (born 1956), clinical psychologist, (Vicksburg)

Arthur Guyton (1919–2003), wrote the *Textbook of Medical Physiology*, (Oxford)

John Hall, continues to work on Textbook of Medical Physiology[27]

James Hardy (1918–2003), surgeon who performed the first successful cadaveric lung transplant, (Jackson)[28]

T. R. M. Howard (1908–1976), surgeon and activist, (Mound Bayou)

Thomas Naum James (born 1925), cardiologist, (Amory)

T. R. M. Howard (1908–1976), surgeon and activist, (Mound Bayou)

Thomas Naum James (born 1925), cardiologist, (Amory)

Politicians

Thomas Abernethy (1903–1998), U.S. representative, (Eupora)

Robert H. Adams (1792–1830), U.S. senator, (Natchez)

James L. Alcorn (1816–1894), governor and U.S. senator, (Friars Point)

William Allain (born 1928), governor, (Washington)

John Mills Allen (1846–1917), U.S. representative, (Tishomingo County)

Apuckshunubbee (c.1740–1824), Choctaw chief

Haley Barbour (born 1947), governor, (Yazoo City)

Ethelbert Barksdale (1824–1893), U.S. representative and member of the Confederate States Congress, (Jackson)

William Barksdale (1821–1863), U.S. congressman, (Jackson)

Ross Barnett (1898–1987), governor, (Standing Pine)

Cheri Barry (born c.1955), mayor, (Meridian)

Marion Barry (born 1936), Washington, D.C. mayor, (Itta Bena)

Theodore G. Bilbo (1877–1947), governor and U.S. senator, (Poplarville)

Marsha Blackburn (born 1952), U.S. representative from Tennessee, (Laurel)

Hale Boggs (1914–1972), U.S. representative from Louisiana, House majority leader, (Long Beach)

David R. Bowen (born 1932), U.S. representative, (Houston)

Walker Brooke (1813–1869), U.S. senator, (Vicksburg)

Blanche Bruce (1841–1898), U.S. senator

Ezekiel S. Candler, Jr. (1862–1944), U.S. representative, (Corinth)

Joseph W. Chalmers (1806–1853), U.S. senator, (Holly Springs)

Travis W. Childers (born 1958), U.S. representative, (Booneville)

John Claiborne (1809–1884), U.S. representative, (Natchez)

Robert G. Clark, Jr. (born 1928), first African American state representative since Reconstruction

Thad Cochran (born 1937), U.S. senator, (Pontotoc)

James P. Coleman (1914–1991), governor, (Ackerman)

Jacqueline Y. Collins (born 1949), Illinois state senator, (McComb)

Ross A. Collins (1880–1968), U.S. representative, (Collinsville)

William M. Colmer (1890–1980), U.S. representative, (Moss Point)

Greg Davis (born 1966), mayor, (Southaven)

Jefferson Davis (1808–1889), U.S. senator and president of the Confederate States of America, (Warren County)

Wayne Dowdy (born 1943), chairman of the Mississippi Democratic Party, (Magnolia)

Brad Dye (born 1933), lieutenant governor, (Charleston)

James Eastland (1904–1986), U.S. senator, (Sunflower)

Mike Espy (born 1953), U.S. secretary of agriculture, (Yazoo City)

Robert C. Farrell (born 1936), Los Angeles city councilman, (Natchez)

Erik R. Fleming (born 1965), state representative, (Clinton)

Kirk Fordice (1934–2004), governor, (Vicksburg)

Webb Franklin (born 1941), U.S. representative, (Greenwood)

Evelyn Gandy (1920–2007), lieutenant governor, (Hattiesburg)

James Z. George (1826–1897), U.S. senator, (Carrollton)

Charles H. Griffin (1926–1989), U.S. representative, (Utica)

Gregg Harper (born 1956), U.S. representative, (Jackson)

Pat Harrison (1881–1941), U.S. representative, (Crystal Springs)

Patrick Henry (1843–1930), U.S. representative, (Brandon)

Thomas C. Hindman (1828–1868), U.S. representative from Arkansas, (Ripley)

Jon Hinson (1942–1995), U.S. representative, (Tylertown)

David Holmes (1769–1832), first Governor of Mississippi Jim Hood, Attorney General of Mississippi, (New Houlka)

Delbert Hosemann (born 1947), Mississippi secretary of state, (Vicksburg)

Benjamin G. Humphreys (1808–1882), governor, (Claiborne County)

Benjamin G. Humphreys II (1865–1923), U.S. representative, (Claiborne County)

William Y. Humphreys (1890–1933), U.S. representative, (Greenville)

Paul B. Johnson, Sr. (1880–1943), judge/governor, (Hattiesburg)

Paul B. Johnson, Jr. (1916–1985), governor, (Hattiesburg)

Pete Johnson (born 1948), state auditor, co-chair of Delta Regional Authority, (Clarksdale)

Daryl Jones (born 1955), (Jackson)

Penne Percy Korth (born 1942), diplomat, (Hattiesburg)

L.Q.C. Lamar (1825–1893), U.S. senator and supreme court justice, (Oxford)

Greenwood LeFlore (1800–1865), Choctaw chief, state senator Clinton LeSueur (born 1969), (Holly Springs)

Elmer Litchfield (1927–2008), sheriff of East Baton Rouge Parish in Louisiana, (Meridian)

Mamie Locke (born 1954), Virginia state senator, (Brandon)

Trent Lott (born 1941), U.S. senator, (Grenada)

John R. Lynch (1847–1939), first African-American speaker of the Mississippi House, U.S. representative, (Natchez)

Ray Mabus (born 1948), governor and Secretary of the Navy, (Starkville)

Harlan Majure (born 1929), mayor of Philadelphia, Mississippi, (Meridian)

Glenn McCullough (born 1954), mayor of Tupelo, (Tupelo)

Chris McDaniel (born 1971), state senator, (Laurel)

Hernando Money (1839–1912), U.S. senator, (Carrollton)

"Sonny" Montgomery (1920–2006), U.S. representative, (Meridian)

Mike Moore (born 1952), Mississippi attorney general, (Pascagoula)

Ronnie Musgrove (born 1956), governor, (Tocowa)

Spencer Myrick (1918–1991), Louisiana legislator, (Simpson County)

Alan Nunnelee (born 1958), state senator, (Tupelo)

Chip Pickering (born 1963), U.S. representative, (Laurel)

John E. Rankin (1882–1960), U.S. representative, (Itawamba County)

Red Shoes (died 1747), assassinated Choctaw leader Bill Renick (born 1954), mayor, governor's chief of staff (Ashland)

Hiram Rhodes Revels (1827–1901), first African-American U.S. senator, (Claiborne County)

Carol Schwartz (born 1944), District of Columbia politician, (Greenville)

Abram M. Scott (1785–1833), governor, (Wilkinson County)

Ronnie Shows (born 1947), U.S. representative, (Moselle)

Jim Singleton (born 1931), New Orleans councilman (Hazlehurst)

Larkin I. Smith (1944–1989), U.S. representative, (Poplarville)

Larry Speakes (born 1939), presidential spokesman, (Cleveland)

John C. Stennis (1901–1995), U.S. senator, (De Kalb)

Bill Stone (born 1965), state senator, (Ashland)

William V. Sullivan (1857–1918), U.S. representative and senator, (Winona)

Gene Taylor (born 1953), U.S. representative, (Bay St. Louis)

Bennie Thompson (born 1948), U.S. representative, (Bolton)

Jacob Thompson (1810–1885), U.S. representative, secretary of the interior, (Oxford)

Amy Tuck (born 1963), lieutenant governor, (Maben)

James K. Vardaman (1861–1930), governor, U.S. Senator, (Yalobusha County)

Jamie L. Whitten (1910–1995), U.S. representative, (Cascilla)

Roger Wicker (born 1951), U.S. senator, (Pontotoc)

Thomas Hickman Williams (1801–1851), U.S. senator, (Pontotoc County)

William Arthur Winstead (1904–1995), U.S. representative, (Philadelphia)

William Winter (born 1923), governor, (Grenada)

Fielding L. Wright (1895–1956), governor, (Rolling Fork)

Supercentenarians

Susie Gibson (1890–2006), lived 115 years & 108 days, (Corinth)

Moses Hardy (1893/1894–2006), lived 112 to 113 years, (Aberdeen)

Bettie Wilson (1890–2006), lived 115 years & 153 days

[edit] Writers

Ace Atkins (born 1970), (Oxford)

Howard Bahr (born 1946), (Jackson)

Frederick Barthelme (born 1943), novelist and professor, (Hattiesburg)

Earl W. Bascom (1906–1995), (Columbia)

Lerone Bennett, Jr. (born 1928), editor of Ebony magazine, (Clarksdale)

Douglas A. Blackmon (born 1964), journalist and historian, (Leland)

Maxwell Bodenheim (1892–1954), poet and novelist, (Hermanville)

Bruce Brady (1934?–2000), writer, editor of Outdoor Life, (Brookhaven)[29]

Charlie Braxton, poet and author, (McComb)[30]

Larry Brown (1951–2004), (Oxford)

Jill Conner Browne, author Sweet Potato Queen, (Tupelo)

Jack Butler (born 1944), (Alligator)

Mary Cain (1904–1984), journalist, (Pike County)

Hodding Carter II (1907–1972), journalist, (Greenville)

Hodding Carter III (born 1935), journalist, (Greenville)

Craig Claiborne (1920–2000), food writer, (Sunflower)

Mart Crowley (born 1935), playwright, (Vicksburg)

Borden Deal (1922–1985), novelist and short story writer, (Pontotoc)

Ben Domenech (born 1981), conservative writer and blogger, (Jackson)

David Herbert Donald (1920–2009), historian, (Goodman)

Ellen Douglas (Josephine Haxton) (born 1921), novelist, (Greenville)[31]

John T. Edge, food writer, (Oxford)

John Faulkner (1901–1963), plain-style writer, (Ripley)

William Faulkner (1897–1962), Nobel laureate, (New Albany)

Bill Fitzhugh (born 1957), (Jackson)[32][33]

Vic Fleming (born 1951), (Jackson)

Shelby Foote (1916–2005), historian and novelist, (Greenville)

Charles Henri Ford (1913–2002), poet, novelist, editor (Brookhaven)

Richard Ford (born 1944), Pulitzer Prize-winning novelist and short story writer, (Jackson)

Lynn Franklin (born 1922), author, police detective

Ellen Gilchrist (born 1935), novelist/poet/short story writer, (Vicksburg)

John Grisham (born 1955), legal thrillers novelist, (Southaven)

Barry Hannah (born 1942), novelist and short story writer, (Clinton)

Charlaine Harris (born 1951), mystery author, (Tunica)

Thomas Harris (born 1940), author who created the character Hannibal Lecter, (Rich)

Beth Henley (born 1952), playwright and screenwriter, (Jackson)

M. Carl Holman (1919–1988), author/poet/playwright, (Minter City)

Greg Iles (born 1960), novelist, (Natchez)

Greg Keyes (born 1963), science fiction and fantasy writer, (Meridian)

Muna Lee (1895–1965), author and poet, (Raymond)

Sam Chu Lin (1939–2006), journalist, (Greenville)

C. Liegh McInnis (born 1969), poet/short story writer/editor of Black Magnolias (Clarksdale)

Anne Moody (born 1940), author, activist, (Centreville)

Willie Morris (1934–1999), author, editor (Jackson)

Jess Mowry (born 1960), writer of books and stories for children and young adults, (Starkville) Ellis Nassour (born 1941), author of non-fiction books, journalist, playwright, formerly with New York Times, (Vicksburg)

Thomas Naylor (born 1936), author and economist, (Jackson)

Lewis Nordan (born 1939), (Forest)

Steven Ozment (born 1939), historian, (McComb)

Walker Percy (1916–1990), (Greenville)

William Alexander Percy (1885–1942), (Greenville)

William Raspberry (born 1935), public affairs columnist, (Okolona)

Kevin Sessums (born 1956), magazine editor, (Forest)

Patrick D. Smith (born 1927), Pulitzer Prize and Nobel Prize nominee, (Mendenhall)

Lynne Spears (born 1955), author and mother of Britney Spears and Jamie Lynn Spears, (McComb)

Elizabeth Spencer (born 1921), novelist, (Carrollton)

Kathryn Stockett, novelist, (Jackson)

William N. Still, Jr. (born 1932), maritime historian, (Columbus)

Donna Tartt (born 1963), novelist, (Greenwood)

Clifton Taulbert (born 1945), author and speaker, (Glen Allan)

Mildred Taylor (born 1943), author, (Jackson)

Wright Thompson (born 1977), journalist, ESPN.com Natasha Trethewey (born 1966), 2007 Pulitzer Prize poet, (Gulfport)

Jamie Langston Turner (born 1949), Christian novelist Brenda Venus (born 1947), author, (Biloxi)

Howard Waldrop (born 1946), science fiction author, (Houston)

Robert W. Walker, novelist, (Corinth)

Peggy Webb (born 1942), romance novel author, (Mooreville)

Eudora Welty (1909–2001), novelist, short story writer (Jackson)

Neil White (born 1960), playwright, publisher, (Gulfport)[34]

Tennessee Williams (1911–1983), (Columbus)

Richard Nathaniel Wright (1908–1960), (Roxie)

Al Young (born 1939), poet/novelist/essayist/screenwriter, (Ocean Springs)

Stark Young (1881–1963), playwright/novelist/literary critic/essayist, (Como)

Other people

Arthur Blessitt (born 1940), preacher, most famous for carrying a cross through every nation of the world, (Greenville)

Miriam Chamani (born 1943), Mambo Priestess and co-founder of the New Orleans Voodoo Spiritual Temple, (Jackson)

James Copeland (1823–1857), outlaw and co-leader of the Wages and Copeland Clan, (Jackson County)

Cat Cora (born 1967), only female Iron Chef America in franchise history, (Jackson)

James A. Ford (1911–1968), archaeologist, (Water Valley)

Fred Haise (born 1933), former NASA astronaut, (Biloxi)

Elizabeth Lee Hazen (1885–1975), microbiologist who contribution in the development of nystatin, (Rich)

Larry Hoover (born 1950), leader of the Gangster Disciple Nation gang, (Jackson)

Leslie Hubricht (1908–2005), biologist and malacologist, (Meridian)

Mary Comfort Leonard (1856–1940), founder of the Delta Gamma Fraternity, (Kosciusko)

L.H. Musgrove (died 1868), outlaw hanged by a vigilante committee in Denver, Colorado, (Panola County)

Haller Nutt (1816–1864), planter, builder of Longwood, (Jefferson County)

Lenny Skutnik (born 1953), celebrity rescuer of 1982 disaster victim

Roy A. Tucker (born 1951), astronomer, (Jackson)

References

^ Local People by John Dittmer, retrieved on 2009-08-08

^ Southern Echo: Dianna Freelon-Foster

^ "Inventory of the Ed King Collection". http://www.olemiss.edu/depts/general_library/archives/finding_aids/MUM00251.html. Retrieved 2009-06-20.

^ Dallas Voice retrieved 2009-08-09

^ "Profile for Rick Anderson". http://www.rickandersonart.com/. Retrieved 2008-07-27.

^ The Meridian Star newspaper: Backstage Pass: Meridian Museum of Art Around Mississippi 2008

^ "William N. Beckwith: biography". http://www.williamnbeckwith.com/biography.html. Retrieved 2009-05-02.

^ University of Mississippi: Notable alumni in Art

^ It runs in the family "Mississippi Magazine". http://www.highbeam.com/doc/1G1-114981882.html?title= It runs in the family. Retrieved 2010-03-25.

^ It runs in the family "Mississippi Magazine". http://www.highbeam.com/doc/1G1-114981882.html?title= It runs in the family. Retrieved 2010-03-25.

^ Mississippi Public Broadcasting: MPB-TV provides LIVE broadcast of 2006 Cellular South Conerly Trophy Presentation

^ "Photographer reflects". http://www.olemiss.edu/depts/south/register/fall04/seven.htm. Retrieved 2009-06-07.

^ "Profile for William Dunlap". http://www.williamdunlap.com/bio/bio.html. Retrieved 2008-07-27.

^ University of Mississippi Dept. of Art Alumni: William Dunlap

^ Paul Grootkerk, "The Visionary Paintings of Theora Hamblett," *Women's Art Journal* 11 (Autumn 1990-Winter 1991): 19-22

^ EdMcGowin.com

^ University Press of Mississippi: Ed McGowin

^ "Ethel Wright Mohamed: biography". http://www.mamasdreamworld.com/bio.htm. Retrieved 2009-05-01.

^ Smithsonian Magazine: Mississippi Cultural Destinations

^ "Profile for Ken Sessums". http://www.jkimsessums.com/bio.html. Retrieved 2008-07-27.

^ Pearl River Community College

^ The Juco Classic New Service

^ "Sam Haskell: 'Promises I Made My Mother'". http://www.msnbc.msn.com/id/30440612/page/2/. Retrieved 2009-06-20.

^ Magnolia Political Report 17

^ "Kenneth Haxton: A Mississippi Musician and Writer". http://www.mswritersandmusicians.com/musicians/kenneth-haxton.html. Retrieved 2009-06-20.

^ Hoyt Ming and His Pep Steppers, by Eugene Chadbourne

^ "Profile for John Hall". http://www.mississippibelieveit.com. Retrieved 2008-07-27.

^ "James Hardy, Surgeon Who Paved Way for Transplants, Dies at 84". *The New York Times*. 2003-02-21. http://www.nytimes.com/2003/02/21/obituaries/21HARD.html. Retrieved 2009-06-20. [dead link]

^ "Bruce Brady Profile". http://www.bradybronze.com/bruce.htm. Retrieved 2009-06-20.

^ "AKR Author: Charlie Braxton". http://www.iveknownrivers.org/authors/author.php?a=Charlie+Braxton. Retrieved 2009-01-16.

^ "Ellen Douglas, Mississippi author". http://www.mswritersandmusicians.com/writers/ellen-douglas.html. Retrieved 2009-06-20.

^ "Bill Fitzhugh's Profile". http://www.billfitzhugh.com/about.html. Retrieved 2008-07-27.

^ "Bill Fitzhugh, Mississippi writer from Jackson". http://www.mswritersandmusicians.com/writers/bill-fitzhugh.html. Retrieved 2009-06-20.

^ "Neil White, Mississippi author". http://www.mswritersandmusicians.com/writers/neil-white.html. Retrieved 2010-04-05.